"Who a

The harsh words caused Emma to spin around.
There was a *big* man leaning over her. A big,
black-haired man with dark eyes and a deep
tan.

"Well, I— Who are *you?*" Emma challenged,
struggling to control herself. There was
definitely something about this man that
disturbed her.

"I asked you first," he said. But when she didn't
respond, he answered impatiently, "I happen to
be the conservator of this place. My name is
Weld. John Weld. And who might you be?"

"I'm just Emma," she replied.

"Emma what?" he demanded. There was a
fierceness to his tone and his eyes glared at her.

"Emma Ballentine," she almost whispered.

The man straightened up and stepped away
from her. "Just what we need. With all
the troubles we have, here comes another
Emma Ballentine."

Emma Goldrick was born and raised in Puerto Rico, where she met and married her husband, Bob, a career military man. Thirty years and four children later they retired and took up nursing and teaching. In 1980 they turned to collaborative writing. The couple's first submission was accepted and they have never looked back. The Goldricks enjoy spending time with their grandchildren when they're not writing, reading or traveling.

Books by Emma Goldrick

HARLEQUIN ROMANCE
3134—MISSISSIPPI MISS
3164—A TOUCH OF FORGIVENESS
3188—DOUBLY DELICIOUS
3303—BABY MAKES THREE

HARLEQUIN PRESENTS PLUS
1576—THE WIDOW'S MITE
1608—SUMMER STORMS

HARLEQUIN PRESENTS
1465—SILENCE SPEAKS FOR LOVE
1488—SMUGGLER'S LOVE
1520—LOVEABLE KATIE LOVEWELL
1545—SPIRIT OF LOVE
1681—THE UNMARRIED BRIDE

Don't miss any of our special offers. Write to us at the following address for information on our newest releases.

Harlequin Reader Service
U.S.: 3010 Walden Ave., P.O. Box 1325, Buffalo, NY 14269
Canadian: P.O. Box 609, Fort Erie, Ont. L2A 5X3

THE BALLEYMORE BRIDE
Emma Goldrick

Harlequin Books

TORONTO • NEW YORK • LONDON
AMSTERDAM • PARIS • SYDNEY • HAMBURG
STOCKHOLM • ATHENS • TOKYO • MILAN
MADRID • WARSAW • BUDAPEST • AUCKLAND

To my daughter Jeanne, without whom I
could never have finished this fantasy

ISBN 0-373-03335-4

THE BALLEYMORE BRIDE

Copyright © 1994 by Emma Goldrick.

CHAPTER ONE

'AND you say that's all he left?'' Emma turned in a circle and scanned the tiny room, the worn furnishings, the rusty sink in the corner. Outside the dingy window she could see the dilapidated nearby buildings of the south Bronx.

"That's all there was, dearie." The landlady was in a hurry. As bad as the room was, it was rentable. "Oh, I almost forgot. There's a suitcase down in the basement. And a package of them queer paintings he did. I'll have Frank bring them up. You won't forget he owed me rent."

"Of course," Emma said. "I'll pay you now." She opened her purse.

"A fine man, he was, Mr. Ballentine," the landlady simpered as she snatched at the offered bills. "You won't be in the room too long?"

Emma brushed her long red hair back off her face. "I don't suppose so."

"You was related?"

"My father," Emma said.

My father, Emma repeated the words to herself. This was the man who left me at the Social Services building when I was five. I cried for him to take me with him, but he didn't.

"I haven't seen him for ten years or more. Where——?"

"The city buried him, miss. I don't exactly know where. In Potter's Field, I s'pose." With her money in

5

hand, her conscience clear, the landlady bustled out of the door.

Emma collapsed on the rickety bed. So much for Edward Everett Ballentine, she thought. He was a good man, they say. I wish I could have known him. Somehow or another, all the dreams she'd had growing up had centered on him coming to get her. He'd come to see her, once, the day she graduated from high school. He'd come to the ceremony and then walked away. He hadn't spoken to her but she'd recognized him, even from a distance. She hadn't called out or gone after him. He was a stranger. He wasn't the "father" she'd built in her daydreams. But he was her *father*.

Much later, when she'd thought about it, she'd realized he must have kept track of her somehow. How else would he have known about her graduation? Or how would he have known where to send that birthday card for her fifteenth birthday? Or even that letter he'd sent when she was sixteen. She'd sworn that she would never read the letter. Heaven only knew what she'd hoped to find in it. Understanding, perhaps, or an invitation to join him. The letter had had neither. She had spent so many years not understanding what she'd done wrong; why he had deserted her. As the years passed and she'd come to understand the letter he'd written, she'd got angry. She kept it safe in her strong box. She couldn't understand why she took such care of it, but she did.

He had sent her another letter. Her finger toyed with the smudged letter in the pocket of her jacket. Written in pencil, addressed to her Staten Island address, the one from which she had moved three years earlier. Uncle Sam and his postmen had finally tracked her down. She pulled out the envelope and took the single sheet of paper out of it again. There was only a single bulb hanging from the ceiling. Emma reached for her gold-rimmed glasses.

"Emma," the letter said. "I haven't done well by you. But others will. Go to Balleymore."

And no signature. She tapped her fingers on the edge of the paper. Through all the years of foster homes, and state care, when she'd needed something or someone, she would have jumped at the chance to know about Balleymore. But now, with her fourth novel on the stands, there was no need.

Balleymore? Where had she heard the name? A long time ago. There was something to do with a house high on a hill, deep in the country, where the snow in winter piled as high as a little girl's head. An old house, and people who walked solemnly and quietly and brushed her out of the way. Where?

There was something painful about the memory, and she could not tell just what it was. She closed her green eyes and thought. Balleymore. Had her father come from there? Or perhaps her mother. Everyone had a mother, even if one didn't remember her. Isn't that strange? she thought. I can remember almost everything. But not my mother. Or Balleymore. Where?

Who am I? she asked herself. Who am I really? There's nothing of me in the world, except for the last four years when my books began to appear on the shelves. Surely somewhere, somehow there are people who know who I am, or who I used to be—and I have to find them! I can't go on any longer without the answers to the question, Who am I?

She tapped the little packet of papers, sealed in plastic, that her father had left behind, but was too tired to investigate them at the moment. They dropped into her

capacious bag as her eyes made one last survey of her
father's domain.

The trip west from Boston was a delight. Her rented
Buick responded like a charm on the fine highways
leading westward. As she approached the rolling hills
around the Mohawk trail, Emma began to look carefully for the sign. Just getting here had appeared impossible, but had turned out to be so easy. How did you
find a house when you didn't know the address? A house
that was only a name? Sitting in her hotel room in New
York, she had been struck quickly by a thought. How
did you find anything? Anybody? You hired a detective!

So, she'd dialed the Trentmore detective agency, expecting a laugh and a big brush-off. Instead, the next
day, she had received a call from the agency and a bright-
sounding man had laughed when he'd told her, "Our
charges for four hours' work are two hundred and fifty
dollars."

Emma had taken a deep breath, her first in some
hours. At least my bank account isn't going to run
aground, she'd thought. "And what did you have to
do?" she had asked.

"Simple," the young man had replied. "We looked
in the National Register of Historical Structures, and,
after considerable searching, there it was. Balleymore,
you said. It's in the hills of western Massachusetts.
General Ephram Ballentine of the Massachusetts Militia
lived there in 1768. Would you like the address and
description?"

Emma would. She had copied all the information
quickly, thanked the young man politely, and sent him
his check before she'd read her notes. The next day, after
a long and violent argument with both her agent and

her editor, she had taken the shuttle flight to Boston, her mind clear for once in a long time. Well, not exactly clear. Her editor had blackmailed her into a promise. One more of those Emma Ballentine thrillers, based in the mountains of the Bay State.

A passing truck, doing seventy miles an hour in a fifty-five-mile zone, sounded its horn and brought her back to attention. The road signs were flashing by. She slowed down to make sure she didn't overlook one of them. Finally, she found the one she was looking for.

Balleymore, the historical marker said, with an arrow pointing north, toward the foothills. She turned off the main highway and within minutes was climbing up and down hills, ridge after ridge, each one rising slightly higher than the one before. The road narrowed, first to three lanes, and then to two. When she came to the turn at the top of the last ridge there it was. "Balleymore," the sign said.

There was a small metal historical marker, such as one saw everywhere in the countryside in New England. Emma pulled over to the side of the road and shifted into neutral. She had not realized how tense she had become. Her shoulders ached, and her eyes were blurring. She set the emergency brake, climbed out of the car and walked over to the marker, glad to be able to stretch her legs.

"Balleymore," the sign said, "the home of General Ephram Ballentine. Revolutionary War General killed in the Battle of Ticonderoga."

Emma leaned against the sign and brushed at her forehead. She had dressed conservatively for this trip, not knowing who or what she might find. Her navy blue suit was perhaps too heavy for the heat of the day, and her hair, fastened up in a tight bun, was beginning to slip its pins. Ephram Ballentine, she thought. Certainly a relative of some sort. And if he isn't, I'm going to claim him anyway! And with that smart conclusion she took off her glasses and headed back toward the car, wiping her eyes.

Not all Massachusetts drivers were insane. But there were enough to give the state a bad name. Just as she reached the front of her car a three-toned horn screamed at her, and a low white two-passenger sports car went by her at rocket speed. Emma was so startled that she dropped both glasses and tissue. Although the road was paved, a dust storm surrounded her, leaving her coughing.

Emma was a tall, healthy girl. She stood five feet eleven in her stockinged feet, weighed in at one hundred and thirty well-curved pounds, and was as blind as a bat without her glasses. She also owned a small but effective vocabulary—perhaps not suitable for New England ladies, but highly desirable for a woman who dealt with fiction editors daily.

By the time she recovered her spectacles they were too dirty to see through. Emma slid into the driver's seat of her car and fished around for her spare set. An old pair, not the lightweight gold-rims she favored, but rather a heavy plastic pair of horn-rims. A few more words for the driver of the little white car, a moment or two to do something about her falling hair, and she started on down the road. And there was the house, popping up out of a sharp turn. It was like nothing she had ever expected to see. All along her mind had been on 1768 and log cabins. Instead, Balleymore was a two-story house, with the central section built of stone like a fortress, with frame additions on each side in the shape of the letter U. Like most New England country houses it was painted white. Sitting atop the central section, squarely over the front door, was a tiny cupola.

She slowed to a stop again. The two extensions that formed the U looked like a pair of welcome arms. Dazed, Emma began to daydream again. The space between the arms was big enough to form a courtyard into which a coach and four would easily fit. With eyes half closed she pictured herself descending from just such a coach. And just at that moment that white sports car came roaring down the hill at her again, its horn tooting wildly as it passed her with no more than inches to spare.

Emma ducked. It seemed to only sensible thing to do. As a result, she failed to see the driver and passenger, both of whom were laughing at her. Stop, Emma commanded herself. Turn around and go back. This is no place for you! She banged her hands on the steering wheel in frustration. And then her common sense took over. Of course this is a place good enough for me, she thought. I hope.

Her fingers were still shaking. She locked them around the steering wheel and drove up into the courtyard. There was deep silence around the house, as if nothing lived in the area. A driveway led around the house to what was evidently a garage—or perhaps merely a converted barn. But nothing stirred there either. Despite the beauty of the place, Emma came down out of her cloud of enjoyment and slapped reality in the face. Nobody here. I can't remember when I last passed a town, she thought. If there's no one on top of this mountain then I'll have to go and find a place to spend the night. Well, I've come this far. Only a coward quits within sight of the enemy. Which was a quotation out of the worst Napoleon Bonaparte book she had ever read. She opened the car door and stepped out, slamming the door lustily hoping someone would hear. Somebody did.

Two dogs came racing around the side of the house, Dobermann pinschers, black as night and as evil as sin, their teeth gleaming at her as they came howling up the driveway.

Emma, not noticeably affected by animal angers, was taken completely by surprise. She backed away from them in the direction of the house. They came snarling, close to her but not up to her. Pawing the ground, both of them with sparkling teeth which looked capable of sheer destruction, they bellied closer. The farther she backed, the more distressed she became. Finally she was cornered in the little niche that led to the front door. She banged on the door a couple of times with no response. The dogs stayed their distance but growled and barked at her. There had to be some other way to get attention. She searched carefully, keeping one eye on the dogs, but there was no doorbell button. There was no knocker, either.

Instead, by the side of the door there was a long steel chain hanging down between two brackets. Emma grabbed the chain, gave it a large pull and then covered her ears when bells began to ring. Heavy bells, loud bells. Coming from the little steeple at the top of the house rather than inside. In a moment, the door opened halfway. Just wide enough for a teenage girl's face to be seen.

"Whatcha want?" the girl asked.

"W-well, the dogs——" Emma stammered. "Let me in, please."

"Not me," the girl said. "I ain't gonna open the door for them damn dogs."

"If you don't, I don't know what's going to happen," Emma said. "I——"

At that moment another voice sounded in the background, "Hilda, what's going on out there?" The door opened a little wider. Beside the thin string of a girl, perhaps sixteen years old, there was now a rounded well-aged woman with gray hair, a gaunt expression and a sense of command about her. She took one look at the person at the door, stepped out on the porch and flapped her apron at the two dogs.

"Shoo, shoo," she said, "you monsters. Shoo!" The dogs reluctantly withdrew.

"Now then," said the lady as she returned to Emma. "I'm Mrs. Macrae, the housekeeper, and you are——" She paused for a second. Her eyes looked as if they were about to jump out of her head. "Emma? Emma, is it you?"

"I—er—yes, I'm Emma. Who—I don't know who you might be. I need to get in. I need to—— Those dogs have scared me nearly to death."

"Come in, child," the housekeeper said. "Come in. Now then, you, Hilda, go heat some water for tea. The girl is shaking to the bone. Shivering in the middle of August, no less. Come here, Emma." She opened her arms wide and Emma, not knowing why, walked into them and received a hug that was well worth the coming. "Emma, Emma, Emma," said the old lady. "It's been so many years. Where have you been, child?"

"I—I'm afraid I don't know where I've been, and I don't really know where I am," Emma stuttered. "I was looking for—is this home?"

"Yes," said the housekeeper comfortingly, "this is home. Come on in, dear." She lead the way into the dark hall and closed the big oak door behind them. It slammed with a satisfying thud that shut out all the troubles and noises of the world.

"Ah, lass, it's good to see you. Come, now, into the lounge where we can sit and talk for a while." They walked down the dark hall to the last door at the back of the house. Mrs. Macrae opened it and they entered the sunshine and glory of a beautiful room. A whole wall of window glass sprayed the sunshine into the room. It was a library as well as a lounge. Books were stacked on three sides, sky-high. A fireplace was in the middle of the north wall. Ornate but unused.

"Sit you here," said the housekeeper. "Here now, Emma, my Emma."

"How do you know me?" Emma asked. "I've never been here before."

"Well, go on with you, lass," the housekeeper said. "Did I not raise you? Did I not change your diapers? Wash you, walk you, talk to you? For four long years were you not the center of my heart? Until he took you away."

"When I was four?"

"When you were four, love. And there's not a change in you, is there, except that you're bigger? Green eyes, I never forgot those big green eyes. And that tawny hair. Only you should let it be free, girl, not bobbed all up in a bunch like an old lady. Now then. You must be hungry. It's been a long time you've been traveling?"

"Well," Emma said, "I flew into Boston from New York this morning and then drove out here. And——"

"No wonder you're tired," the housekeeper said. "No wonder you're shaking. Sit you down here. Now then, you wait just a minute while I go stir up the kitchen. We'll have a little hot tea and a little something to eat. And then you'll tell me."

Emma sat down. She relaxed for the first time in a long time. She rested her arms on the arms of the chair. It was a strange welcome. To come all these years and all this distance and find somebody who knew you when you were a little girl? Amazing. Yet it was only a part of the search. She relaxed against the back of the chair, slouched slightly to rest herself and closed her eyes for a moment. She was being enveloped by a feeling that she'd never had before. She felt at home and she couldn't explain the feeling. She liked it.

In the distance, a great clock was booming. She could count the steady, solemn strokes. Four o'clock in the afternoon.

She heard the door open behind her and straightened up to look over her shoulder. Mrs. Macrae came in with the teenager, who was carrying a tray.

"Put it down here on the table, Hilda," Mrs. Macrae said. "Right there beside the poor girl. And now go you up and make sure that the green room is ready."

The teenager, Hilda, placed the tray on the side table, rattling the cups as she did. Then she nodded her head and disappeared.

"So now, Emma Ballentine," said the housekeeper. "Tea?" She poured a cupful without waiting for acknowledgment and passed it over.

It was warm. Emma cherished the cup between her fingers. Why she was shivering she couldn't tell. Why she felt cold she didn't know. But the warmth of the teacup did something to her. Carefully, she lifted it to her lips, managed to hold it steady for a moment and then sipped.

"Mrs. Macrae—you knew me? You knew me when I was a child?"

"I knew you when you were a child, lass. I did that. I knew your father. How is he?"

"I'm—I'm afraid it's all bad news," Emma said. "My father died three months ago, in New York."

"Ah. Have you been all alone since then?"

"No, it—— Well, I've been alone most of my life," Emma said. "Not just since Father died. I've been all alone since I was five." Mrs. Macrae tried to smother a small muted cry but gave Emma a nod to continue on. "He couldn't support me and I ended up in a state orphanage and half a dozen foster homes." Her audience tsked and shook her head. "But those days are behind me now. I've managed to establish myself in a small business. I never heard of Balleymore until my father sent me a note that told me to come here."

She reached into her wallet and pulled out the crumpled letter her father had left. The housekeeper whipped up her glasses, which were suspended across her bosom by a bright gold chain.

"Ah," she said. "Of course, why should you not? You should have come long, long before." Mrs. Macrae continued under her breath, "You should never have left. I would have cared for you."

Emma wasn't sure she had heard correctly, said, "I didn't even know the place existed."

"Ah, well. We'll make you home here now," Mrs. Macrae said. "Home is the place that's always ready to welcome you back, child. And here we are. All waiting."

"When you say you are all waiting, who is that? Do I have family? Brothers, sisters, aunts or uncles?" Emma asked.

"No," Mrs. Macrae replied with great sympathy. "There's only you in your generation. Your mother and father were only children. The Ballentines were never large families. You are the end of the line.''

"Oh—well. I—this is some strange place," Emma commented, almost trying to change the subject.

"Strange?"

"There's nothing around it. There's no place close. No city. No town."

"Ah," Mrs. Macrae laughed. "'Twas the conceit of the old general, you know. He wanted to be at the frontier, and this was the frontier in those days. Built this house, he did, on the spot where the Indians burned down the old wooden fort. Swore no one would ever do that again. Built it out of stone. And then marched off to war—the Revolution, you ken—and never came back. Famous, famous man."

"I suppose so," Emma said, sighing. "Although I've never heard of him."

Two more sips of the hot tea put her back into constitutional shape. There were little finger sandwiches. Ham, bacon, tomato sandwiches. She sampled one of each and gained her strength back quickly.

"The house seems empty," she offered.

"Oh, not exactly, Emma," Mrs. Macrae said. "Not exactly. There's a lot of living going on behind these walls. Upstairs are the two of them, and down here are Hilda and me and him, who went out to work in the fields today. Working the fields—what I mean is, supervising the work in the fields. He comes several times a week."

Emma nodded her head as if she were an expert. But the other item stuck on her tongue. "Him?"

"Yes, him. Mr. Weld. He does the supervising, you know. There is none here, outside of him, who can make a decision. Him and the lawyers. Although he has been trying to get his brother involved in the farm.''

"Ah," Emma said. "Do they own the place?"

"Oh, no," Mrs. Macrae said. "They just run the place. They—her, upstairs, she owns the place. At least, we think so. And Mr. Weld has been appointed the conservator of the place by the local court. You know she's not well, not well at all. In fact, we hardly ever see her. Ah, but you now. What have you done? Where is your mark on the world, Emma?"

"It's hardly a mark," Emma said. "A scratch maybe. I've written four books that have sold pretty well. Fiction. I don't say that they're world shakers, but two of them have managed to make the *New York Times* bestseller list."

"A writer, now! There had to be some talent in you, of course," she said. "Your mother was a painter. Your father was an artist himself but not as good as she. So now, our Emma is an eminent writer. Well."

"Oh, don't say it like that," Emma said, chuckling. "Eminent? Hardly. Passable, perhaps. I think of myself as a journeyman in the trade. I have a lot to learn. I don't know enough about people, places and things. I don't even know who I am."

"You have come to the right place to find out," Mrs. Macrae said, and then she went quiet.

Emma's eyes were blinking. She struggled to keep them open and failed. The teacup rattled in her hand and was snatched away from her by an unseen rescuer. She leaned back against the chair. "Balleymore," she mumbled, "home?"

There was no more sound to be heard. Her ears had shut down as her mind wrestled with all this new information. All the years of trial and tribulation. All the longing, all the fears and here I am. Do I belong here? she asked herself. Without her notice the day passed by and it was coming on sunset.

Emma had no feeling for time. A door slammed and a heavy voice said something harsh, threateningly. Emma squirmed farther down in the chair, pulling the broken quiet around her like a shield. Suddenly there was a hand on her shoulder shaking her.

"Hey now. Who in God's name are you?"

Emma opened her eyes, with a snap. He shook her again and almost cracked her neck. Her glasses had slipped down her nose. She pushed them back up to bring him in focus. There was a *big* man leaning over her. A big, black-haired man. She blinked her eyes. His face was craggy, the skin tanned from an outdoor life. A line or two marked the brow. His eyes were too close for her to focus. A great deal of sunshine had fallen on that face. The eyes were dark; almost as dark as his hair. The nose was, perhaps, a little too big for the face, but still not out of proportion entirely. And it was altogether too close to her for comfort!

"I say again, who are you?"

"Well—I—— Who are *you*?" Emma challenged, clearing her throat and struggling to get control of herself. There was something about this man that disturbed her; he was more than the sum of his parts.

When Emma didn't respond he shook his head. "I asked you first," he said. When Emma didn't respond he said very slowly, as if to an idiot child, "I happen to be the conservator of this place. My name is Weld. John Weld. And who might you be?"

"Why, I——" Emma stumbled over her words. All of a sudden she felt very small, very unimportant, very weak. "I'm just Emma," she said.

"Emma what?" he demanded. There was a fierceness to his tone and his eyes glared at her. "Emma what?"

Her lips were so dry, she had to moisten them with the tip of her tongue. "Emma—Emma Ballentine," she almost whispered.

The man straightened up and stepped away from her. One step, two steps. "Oh, my God. With all the troubles we have, here comes another Emma Ballentine."

Emma propelled herself to her feet, shaking more now than when she had first arrived. "What do you mean, *another* Emma Ballentine?" she snapped.

"Very simple," he said. "The lawyers are coming this week. Emma Ballentine may very well inherit a lot of property. Not much money, you understand, but the property is quite valuable. You are the second claimant to the throne. Which mouse hole did you pop out of, lady?"

Emma clenched both her fists. I'd love to hit him, she thought, I really would, and he's not that much taller than me. Six feet? Too big to hit, but I could kick him. I have sharp-toed shoes and——

He was watching where she was looking and stepped another step or two away. "No, you don't, lady," he said, and grinned as he said it. "I don't intend to have my shins bruised by another claimant."

At that moment the door opened and Mrs. Macrae came in. "Ah, good evening, John," she said.

"Good evening, Edna," he returned. "Where did we get this one?"

"*This* one just appeared out of the clear blue sky about two hours ago," Mrs. Macrae said. "And, John——?"

"Yes, dear?"

"John, this one is real. I remember her. The dark green eyes, the pixie face, the lovely hair. I remember her well. All those years ago, but she looks just like she did then."

"Come on, now, Edna," he said. "It's a long time ago. A long, long time ago. You remember when she was—what? Four years old?"

"Yes, four years old. I remember her well."

"Well, we have to have more proof than that," he said. "A lot more. In the meantime——"

"In the meantime," Mrs. Macrae said, "I've put her up in the green room, next door to that other—person."

John chuckled. "That other person? You don't trust my brother's protégé?"

"I don't trust him farther than I could throw a piano," Mrs. Macrae said. "Nor her either. Emma was a redhead. From the day she was born she had red hair. Red hair, emerald green eyes, freckles, and a temper to match. This other——" she paused for a moment to mull over a couple of descriptive adjectives and then decided not to use them after all "—and this other one is a dirty blond with light green eyes. You can change your hair color with a little dye, but your eyes don't change. No, this is the one, John. Believe me."

"I don't know what to say," John mused. "I don't remember. I guess I must have been about ten when they—I guess I'll have to leave it to the lawyers. All right. Send her off and get her cleaned up. Let her get bedded down. We'll have them all at dinner, shall we?"

"What a lovely idea," Mrs. Macrae said. "Come on, Emma. Come with me."

She reached out her hand. Emma took it for comfort's sake and edged her way around this big crude man. She hurried to the door, hoping that he wouldn't catch up with her while her back was turned. Mrs. Macrae stopped at the door, patted her hand one time.

"Don't worry about him," Mrs. Macrae murmured. "He has a terrible bark but he never bites. Dinner at seven tonight. We don't dress fancy."

Easy enough for you to say, Emma muttered under her breath as she followed the housekeeper up the stairs.

Her room was at the head of the stairs, in the main section of the house. The green room referred to the décor. A thick green rug, green dimity curtains and the upper half of the walls were finished in a pale green swirl. The bed did not match the room. It was an old brass bedstead, big enough for four. Or five, she told herself as she fell back onto it.

The firm mattress bounced her a couple of times. Emma threw out her arms as far as they would go, and squealed at the joy of relaxation. Two hours, her wristwatch told her. Two hours to relax and puzzle and——

There was another door in the wall. More curious than tired by now, Emma bounced off the bed and tried the knob. The bathroom was almost as big as the bedroom, with a big claw-footed tub, a shower, and all the other appurtenances. "Shower!" she commanded herself.

Her bags had been brought up while she had been napping downstairs. Unpacking was short work. Emma had not yet brought her wardrobe up to the level of her income. What she carried was mostly wash-and-wear, to fit into her heavy travel schedule.

Dinner tonight. Everyone would be present. She had no idea who "everyone" might be. But certainly it would be inspection time, and she the inspectee. From her limited selection she chose a light blue shirtwaister that would hug her bodice, and swing jauntily down to her knees. It was one of those dresses which were advertised as being "wickedly demure." Emma hung it up on the wardrobe door, and dug into her bag for her shower robe and her toilet kit.

Wickedly demure? She had owned the dress for a year, and had yet to have the nerve to wear it in public. It wasn't the sort of thing one would wear to a "book" party, and, outside of her editor and her agent, she hardly knew another male under sixty-five.

But—John Weld? Not perhaps the sort of man for an amateur to try her claws on. On the other hand, he *was* the only male in residence. And a girl, she lectured herself, who has dreamed for years about marriage and a home and children had darned well better get on her track shoes! And so into the shower.

There were lots of good reasons to enjoy an old house. On the other hand, there were always possibilities for disaster. Emma approached the shower with caution. It looked fairly new. The chrome was on all the fixtures, and the knobs matched. She turned on the hot-water tap first. It quickly worked up a head of steam, and she mixed in some of the cold and climbed in herself.

There were few joys for a traveler that exceeded the pleasure of slipping into a warm shower. Emma reveled in it, used the soap liberally, and carefully scrubbed herself down. The soft smoothness of her hands matched up against the velvet of her skin. She snatched them away. Life in state care taught sixteen-year-old girls to beware of men—all men.

Just the idea brought a body-wide blush. She shut off the water and climbed hastily out onto the bath mat. A full-length mirror was mounted on the wall directly opposite the shower. Emma used both hands to wipe of steam from its surface. She grabbed for one of the towels on the warming rack, and punished her own insolence with a harsh rubdown. And then into her robe, and a hairbrush for her required one hundred strokes. She took her medicine. Good, she thought as she gagged down the bitter-tasting liquid, I don't have to do this much longer. With that distasteful chore done, she breezed out into the bedroom, followed by a trail of steam.

There was an unusual feeling in her heart—a celebration of youth. Everything had come true—so far—on this expedition into the unknown, she told herself. She knew more about herself now than she had ever known before. And Mrs. Macrae could very well prove to be a wonderful source of information and understanding.

She had lived here at Balleymore. People knew her. She did a couple of pirouettes in the middle of the spacious bedroom, humming as she went. And then she heard the scream!

Bathrobe around her, comb in hand, Emma ran for the door. The scream had come from her right, down the hall at what would be the north wing. Barefoot, Emma sprinted down and around the corner—and ran into a heavy door that blocked off the entire wing.

Emma paused. Because I heard a scream, should I try to break in? Warily her hand tried the knob. It refused to move. A relatively new Yale lock provided the barrier.

So did one knock and say, Who's screaming in there? She put her ear to the door and heard nothing. She backed off a step or two until she was back in the transverse corridor.

"Maybe, Emma Ballentine," she lectured herself, "you could just for once mind your own business?"

*   *   *

John Weld leaned back in his swivel chair and shook his head. The desk in front of him was covered with papers. Wearily he ran one large hand through his hair. There had been enough surprises today. Especially the last one. Emma Ballentine II was some dish!

The door opened and his younger brother Luke came in.

"Well, you look like the cat that found the cream."

"Not exactly. To tell the truth, John, I'm a little short of——"

"Cash? Damn it, Luke, you draw a salary—oh, hell, how much do you need now?"

"About five hundred," his brother said. Brother John knew he was being conned, but was too tired to do anything about it. He fished his wallet out of his back pocket and peeled off the requisite bills.

"You won't regret it, John. When all this mess of paperwork is settled up, you'll see you'll get all your money back."

"You mean that you and Jill——"

"Yep. Me and Jill. It can't be too much longer, can it?"

"I don't think that's the way to talk."

"Come off it. You know that you hate the old woman as much as I do."

"Well, I congratulate you, brother," John said. "Jill's not the brightest girl that ever came down the pike, but you can't beat her for looks. There's only one little problem."

"What's that?"

John gestured toward the scattered pile of papers in front of him. "There's another Emma Ballentine shown up on the scene."

"Oh, my God!"

"My God is right. This one appeared out of a clear blue sky, with a handful of papers. Including her birth certificate, her father's death certificate, and a holograph will. Can you imagine that? According to her, Edward Ballentine died broke in New York City about three months ago."

John had been riffling through the papers. Now he looked up. His brother had turned as pale as a ghost.

"You're not going to fall for that, John?"

"Fall for?" John eased his swivel chair back from the desk and studied his younger brother. Very seldom do you see a working farmer dressed in a white suit, he told himself. Nor one with clean fingernails when he was supposedly overseeing the potato crop. But he had admonished Luke a hundred times or more with no results. At thirty, Luke Weld was not interested in being a farmer. Something else had to be found for him.

"Yeah. A good-looking chick comes along with a stack of papers and——"

"You've got that right. She is one good-looking lady. Listen, we're all dining over here tonight. Better tell Jill. And get out of here now. I've got a million things to do beforehand."

He turned back toward the papers in front of him, but was unable to concentrate. A good-looking chick. Indeed she was. Flashing green eyes, flaming-red hair with a temper to match, and a figure that would stop the show in any hall.

All he had to do was discover which of the two Emmas was the legal heir. This might be harder than he thought, considering the fact that Emma's mother broke up the Weld household. He hated the entire Ballentine family, but he would find the legal heir and dump the estate, with all its problems, on her.

CHAPTER TWO

EMMA came downstairs to dinner following Hilda, who had been sent to guide her. The narrow stairs puzzled her; she hadn't considered them when she had first come up, nor had she paid any attention to the narrow, heavily shuttered windows which pierced the stone walls. Not until she had reached the bottom step did she realize. The original house had been built on the frontier, when every house had also had to serve as a fortress against French, American Indian and British attacks. The thought gave her a shiver and a small insight into the people who lived and worked in this north country.

Her blue dress was also giving her some thought. She shrugged her shoulders trying to settle the garment. It had not quite lived up to her expectations or perhaps she had changed too much in the year or more since she'd bought it. In any event, it was more promising than demure. It clung too closely to the curve of her hips and displayed too much of the top of her breasts. As long as she was uncertain of her position here at Balleymore, she wasn't in any position to make any promises to anyone of any sort. Especially, she thought, to John Weld.

She came to the dining room midway along the corridor where double doors were thrown wide-open. She stood between them for a moment looking in. The room was huge. In fact, the mahogany table, which looked to be able to seat eighteen people, was merely an odd piece of furniture tucked in one corner. There was a fireplace,

27

as in all the other rooms on the ground floor, but this one was massive, with its mantel head-high and its hearth wide enough for six-foot logs. Bottle-glass windows that had been enlarged far beyond their first origins spread the light of the setting sun across the room, breaking that light into prisms of color. A chandelier that once had held two dozen candles was now converted to electricity. The three people in the room were dwarfed by the room and its furnishings.

John Weld came over to meet her at the door, holding out both his hands toward her in genial welcome. For want of knowing what else to do she put her own in them and watched as they were engulfed. A spark ran up and down her spine. He was a big man, no doubt about it. She had to look up to him, and that was strange for a woman of her own height. His face was handsome but just a little ragged: furrows along his brow, a line down each cheek, a set look in his face as if he had been overworking for years. Those dark eyes of his pinned her like a butterfly pinned in a collection. They were the color of mahogany wood and they were inspecting the dress she was wearing. His bronzed skin indicated that he was an outdoor man. Her quick survey confirmed her earlier judgment. John Weld was a man of whom any woman might beware. Another shiver ran up her spine and the blush she was trying to fight climbed to her cheeks.

"Well," he said. His voice was a rumbling bass, somewhat roughened, as if he had done a lot of loud directing in his day.

She waited for something else to come.

He shook his head and chuckled. "Well, just well. You look very well, my dear."

"Well, I—thank you." Not a word about how her figure overcrowded her dress. She gave silent thanks, and her crossed fingers behind her back relaxed. The look he'd given her was enough to set her heart pounding.

"Come and meet these others." He towed her along across the dining room. "My brother Luke."

Emma almost swallowed her tongue. *My brother Luke*? Brother Luke was not as tall as John but he was as well proportioned. Streamlined, in fact. Where John had warm brown eyes, Luke's were gray. Where John had unruly black hair, Luke was a slicked-down blond. Where John's skin was deeply tanned, Luke's was perfectly pearl. Where John's face looked like the face of a man who lived, Luke looked like a man who played at life. Almost totally different, the two brothers. Except that there was something in the eyes, in the shape of the mouth, which showed a relationship. Emma could not quite put her finger on the similarity.

"Luke," John said, "this is Emma Elizabeth."

Emma reached out her hand to the blond man and then was embarrassed because he made no move to take it. He kept his hands glued to his sides. For a moment Emma's hand hung in mid-air until she snatched it back and folded it behind her back.

"Always the diplomat," John murmured sarcastically.

"Emma Elizabeth, is it?" Luke had a half-empty glass in his hand, a large glass. There was no telling how many times it had been refilled, but he smelled of bourbon, and he had the look of one who had been to the well too often.

Stop that, Emma told herself. No prior judgments. He may be just nervous because I'm here. The flu bug may be running around the area—maybe he's just recovering? Or maybe not? The thought hung in the air between them. He's nervous because I'm here? She nodded at him in brief acknowledgment.

"And this," John said, indicating the girl who stood at Luke's side, "is Luke's fiancée. Her name's Emma, too. Emma Jill. But she prefers to be called by her middle name, Jill."

"Do you say so?" said Emma as she reached out her hand again. Her heart wasn't in it. Why is it, she asked herself, that all the bad ones turn out to be so good-looking? I don't understand this at all. There was something in the Bible about things like that, but for the life of her the quotation did not come to mind.

Jill stood about five feet four. A lean but finely shaped body was outlined in an almost transparent green silk dress. It caressed her from bustline to upper thigh, and then flared out into a sweeping skirt that flirted with her knees. Long light strawberry blond hair gleamed in the light as it hung down her back almost to her waist. Light green eyes sparkled like devils. A cute little smile was accompanied by two little dimples. Good Lord, Emma grumbled to herself, if this is the opposition I'm supposed to battle I'm totally disarmed! Please, Lord, give her some sort of imperfection!

"I'm pleased to meet you," Jill said as she put out her hand. Emma gave a sigh of relief. The girl's voice was marred with a strong New England accent which rang flatly around the conversation. Her hand, offered with genuine politeness, had all the consistency of a wet fish.

"Jill," Emma said. "That's an interesting name. Is there some background for it?"

"No. No, no," the girl said, "my father couldn't live with me—his work, you know." Emma nodded her head. She understood that part excessively well. "He hired a couple to take care of me, and then he would come and visit me every month. My foster parents didn't like the name "Emma," so they called me Jill, and when my father died—well, here I am."

"Here you *am* indeed," Emma said as she produced a mini-smile. Well, maybe there's a hope for us tall women, she told herself. There had better be. But why is that? Because these two men astonished her. The resemblance was hard to find. John was the rugged-hewn man of the frontier, big and hardworking. Luke was one of the most polished men she had ever seen in her life. He would easily fit into the most sophisticated society Boston had to offer. It would be difficult to choose between them, Emma thought to herself, but then again, no one is offering me a choice, are they? Well——

At that moment another person came through the door. Emma looked up in surprise. The newcomer was an elderly woman dressed in the stiff starched white of a nurse's uniform. She came forward with mannish strides right up to the group and presented herself. "Harriet Snow," she said.

Emma exchanged handshakes with her and wondered that her hand wasn't crushed by the contact. Jill evidently knew better. She just simpered and nodded her head.

"Now, that completes us," John said. "Shall we sit down to dinner?"

He moved them over to the table. He sat at the head, Emma was on his right and Jill on his left. Luke sat next to Jill and Harriet sat next to Emma. No sooner had they taken their positions when the door to the kitchen swung in and Mrs. Macrae came in pushing a wheeled cart, loaded with steaming dishes.

"Family dinner," the housekeeper said, as she started to place serving dishes in the middle of the table. "You see what you want and you help yourself. A boiled New England dinner for you today."

"That's what I like," John said.

Jill made a small moue. "It must be terribly fattening."

"Only for some of us," Mrs. Macrae replied. She tried to stifle a chuckle while she turned to leave the room. "Only for some of us."

The dinner passed quickly. John led most of the conversation. "First a little something about Jill. Would you believe it, she's been living only sixty miles away from here? Down the Merrimac valley. Practically neighbors, so to speak. Isn't it a wonderful thing that we could find her?"

"Oh, yes," Luke said. He was having trouble articulating. Even drunk, and he had to be by now, he still looked polished. "Lucky I saw the picture and story in the newspaper," he said. Another silence.

"I guess it was good luck," John repeated. "And then, Emma here is from New York. That's another surprise. She comes bearing affidavits."

"And what do you mean by that?" Luke said angrily.

"Why, Emma has a few official papers concerning herself and her family. I'll have to send them all in to the lawyers for consideration," John said. "We'll talk them over later. But how about you, Harriet? How's our patient?"

The nurse shrugged her shoulders. "There's no real progress from day-to-day," she reported. "As you know. But today was bad. Almost as if she feels something developing in the house and it's upsetting her tremendously. I had a hard time putting her down. I'm afraid that continual use of Valium is not going to be the answer.''

"Do you think that Dr. Weston will be over very soon?" John asked.

"He ought to be," the nurse said. "Although I don't see what he could do. I think we've come to the end of the trail, John. We have to recognize that it'll be all downhill from here."

"Oh, my." Emma looked across the table. Jill was dabbing at her eyes with a tiny lace handkerchief. Luke made a clumsy effort to comfort her, moving his chair close, and putting one arm around her. She turned her face into the broad expanse of his shirt and sniffled.

John tapped his finger on the table a couple of times, as if trying to drum his thoughts along. Emma watched that big finger as it thudded repetitively on the polished mahogany. There was something almost hypnotic in the action. And at the same time something of repressed violence. When he spoke, the sound of his voice snapped Emma out of her trance.

"That's good of you, Jill," he said. "Even though you hardly know her. Don't let it get you down. It's probably the easiest way out for her."

"I can't help it," the girl moaned. "It reminds me of when my—my father died. And yesterday, when Luke took me in to meet her, she seemed so nice to me, as if I were some little girl she knew."

"That's true," Nurse Snow reflected. "She normally doesn't have any reaction at all to visitors, but she was nice to Jill." The nurse leaned across the table. "You might do better, child, if you tell us about your father. Sometimes talking about grief makes the pain easier to bear."

"She treated Jill well because she knew she was her daughter," Luke interjected. "That's all we need to settle all this argument. Take this——"

He stopped. His brother was glaring at him; those warm brown eyes had turned very dark, sparking danger signals. Jill stepped into the silence.

"My dad was a wonderful man," she said. Everyone turned toward her. "A gentle man. He did some sort of important work down in Springfield. Then one Sunday he came up to see me, and we went out on the river, canoeing. There was this other boat, with two boys on it." She dabbed at her eyes again. "You know. Horsing around like a pair of fools. The younger one fell overboard, and he couldn't swim. My dad went overboard in a flash, only when he got the kid to where he could hang on to the side of the boat one of those big tree branches came sweeping down on the current. I—never saw my dad again." Full stop for a flood of tears.

Luke gave up on the handkerchief, and picked up one of the pristine white cloth napkins. It helped.

"He never really talked about his family. It was a shock to have Luke show up and say I belonged here. I miss my father. He was a great hero," Jill mumbled.

"Yes, I'm sure he was," John agreed. There was a flood of compassion in his voice as he leaned over to pat one of the little girl's hands.

Woman, Emma told herself. She's not a girl, she's a woman. And either she's the world's best actress, or it really happened. Am *I* the one who's the wrong Emma? After all, I'd never heard of Balleymore until I received that letter. She gnawed at her lower lip and took her eyes off the weeping woman, only to find that John was staring at her with a quizzical look in his eyes. Emma ducked her head away, and for some reason her cheeks flared blush red.

"And how long ago was this?" John asked gently.

"Why, six years ago," Jill replied. "And I had to wear black dresses. I hate black. I'm not going——" The sobs broke through again.

"Don't let it concern you," John said. "You won't have to wear black dresses again." Jill withdrew her head from Luke's shoulder and flashed a tear-strewn smile.

Almost as if, Emma told herself, wearing the black dresses was the worst part of the happening. And then, because the thought was grossly unfair, she managed a weak, apologetic look in Jill's direction.

"And how about *your* father?" John asked Emma.

They were all watching her, and she was embarrassed. Writing was an occupation which even the shy could endure, she knew. You could hide behind your characters, let your emotions well up out of somebody else's brain, and all the while you yourself could lean back and laugh. But not now. They were all staring.

"Emma?" He was going to insist. For some reason he *wanted* to embarrass her! Damn the man! "Emma?"

"I—don't know that much about my father," she mumbled.

"Speak up, girl." A command this time, not a suggestion. She turned and glared at him, wondering if all the hatred she felt was showing.

"We must have left—here—when I was four," she told them defiantly. "Jill and I had something in common. My dad couldn't keep me, either. When I was five he turned me over to the social services. He wasn't able to support me. I bounced around from one foster home to another. Luckily, when I went into high school I found a sympathetic English teacher who directed me into writing. I sold my first book shortly after I graduated. As for my father, I only saw him once after he left me. He came to my graduation from high school. But I only saw him from a distance. All I know about him is that he was a surrealist painter, and that he died about three months ago. He sent me a letter once. I think he'd been drinking when he wrote it. He rambled on saying that he and my mother should never have married. That they were wrong for each other. He kept saying how sorry he was and that, when he made his name, he'd come for me. He didn't realize that painters rarely made their names before their deaths. And of course he never came. Oh, well.''

"You mean he left you nothing?" Luke glared at her from across the table, his perfect face seeming to demand a retraction of such an obvious lie.

She didn't understand his interest, but she answered honestly. "Regrets and old clothes," Emma said. "I took the clothes to the Salvation Army. Oh, he also left me a package of paintings. Surrealist paintings. His pictures looked as if he had painted them while standing in the anteroom of hell. Me, I like the old-fashioned paintings. The ones where you recognize what the artist is painting."

"What did you do with the paintings?" John asked. "Did you keep them in his memory? Or did you throw them out?"

"It was odd. Not long after I got the paintings, I met a fan of mine who owns an art gallery. I handed them over to him and he said he'd sell them for me—on commission, of course. About two weeks ago he sold one of the paintings for twelve thousand dollars and then, just before I came up here, he sold another for fifty thousand dollars. He says that if we leak them on to the market we should be able to sell the remainder for around seventy-five thousand dollars a picture, or higher. He's conducting a campaign to let buyers know the artist is dead. I understand that to be the thing. Only when the artist has passed on can you really assess what his work will bring. Crazy!"

Jill gasped. "You got fifty thousand dollars for one painting? And you expect higher for each of the others? How many others?" she demanded avidly.

"I think I have about twenty of them. It's not a lot to show for a lifetime of work," Emma said, reflectively and a little sadly.

"Did you give all of them to the gallery?" John inquired, as if he wondered about her feelings for the dead artist.

"I only kept one. It was a homely little thing. A picture of a young girl sitting in the grass with her dog at her side. It looked familiar. I decided not to offer it."

That statement put a blanket of silence over the group. They all seemed to be pondering. Emma shrugged her shoulders. Maybe they know more about painting than I do, she told herself. Although the way Jill's lips are moving she's counting up what you have if you sell twenty paintings at seventy-five thousand dollars a piece. And the counting seemed to be difficult. There weren't any more questions, at least, those they were going to ask. People started to eat urgently of the ham, potatoes cooked in ham juice, cabbage, peas, and corn. It was a typical New England farm dinner.

The meal went down well with everyone, except for Jill's voiced consideration for her weight. But, after having made her original statement, the girl ate like a horse. Emma did too, but she had reason. A girl her size took a lot of filling.

It had been a long time since she had sat down to a formal dinner. Orphanages and foster homes seldom ran to such. But finally it was over.

"I'll go back upstairs," the nurse said. "I'll have my coffee later." She fled from the dining room.

Emma looked at John. "Who is it?" she asked. "Who is upstairs?"

John looked at her, and then at the engaged couple on the other side of the table. They were involved in some long-running whispered conversation. "Why don't we go out into the garden for a walk?" he suggested. "I'll tell you all I can."

"That sounds good." Emma started to move from her chair. John was up instantly, pulling the chair back for her so that she could get away from the table. Emma had read a great deal about actions like this, but never before had she been in a position to enjoy the custom. It was pleasing.

Now I know, she thought, what it means to be cosseted. Raised as she had been in an orphanage, and then fostered in several different homes, she had developed into a rough-and-tumble girl—who had grown into a rough-and-tumble woman. But, feeling the glamour of it all, she gently took John's arm in hers and the two of them walked out of the dining room into the back hall.

As soon as they approached the door, the whispering between Luke and Jill stopped and turned almost immediately into a shouting match.

"Does she get to keep it all?" Jill wailed shrilly.

"He's not *your* father," Luke snapped, "so just keep your trap shut!"

Emma was too far away to hear what the rest of the conversation was about, but it certainly was of some importance to the pair of them. Jill's flat shrill voice dominated Luke's deep baritone. Emma stopped for a moment, tugging at John's arm. They paused in the middle of the double doors.

"Is there something I shouldn't have——?" she started to say.

"Don't interrupt," John said. "Just keep on moving, lady." He patted her hand, resting in the crook of his elbow, and locked it in place with his own. He towed her out into the center of the hallway down to the back of the house and out through a pair of screen doors into the garden. Before them was the eastern slope of the mountains. In the west, where the sun was just setting, Emma could see the outline of several little villages. Each of them was pinpointed by its white church spire.

In the far distance, the pristine valley of Williamsburg was painted in the gaudiest colors of sunset. The air was refreshing. It might be filled with acid rain and other things but Emma's nose couldn't register such. Everything smelled wonderfully! The birds were still active in the trees behind the house. They were big trees, remnants of the long past of the area. Down the hill, in front of them, a long way down, the smooth green rows of cultivation marked the farm lands.

"Very nice," she said appreciatively. "Very nice."

"Over here, Emma." John tugged her along with him. He was moving, perhaps a little too fast even for her long legs.

She made a muted protest. He stopped and looked at her, smiled and then moved more slowly. It was the smile that did it. Emma took one good look and then ducked her head away. It was like walking into the middle of the spider's web, she thought. There's always a smile. "Come into my parlor, said the spider." Yeah, and I'm the fly.

And that was the moment when she heard the dogs. The same pair that had come ravening after her at the front porch. Now they swept around the southwest corner of the house, baying at her. If that was what Dobermans did. "Oh, my God!" she screamed, and ducked around John so that he would be between her and the animals. There was a grin on the man's face. A teasing smile.

"They may not eat me," he told her, "but I'm not sure at all about you. If I stand still, maybe I'll be all right?"

"Well, *thank you*, hero," she snapped, doing her best to cling closer, or perhaps even to climb his frame to safety.

But by then the dogs had arrived. They slid to a stop at John's feet, then came to a sitting position, their great tongues lolling out of one side of their mouths.

"Tell them to go away," Emma whispered fiercely at him.

"Okay. Go away, guys." The two dogs looked up at him, snorted, and continued to sit. "They don't understand *go away*."

"If you're teasing me," Emma threatened, "I'm going to give you such a knock!"

"There's nothing to be afraid of," he told her. "The pair of them are well-trained. They won't bite. Well, I take that back. They did bite my brother a couple of years back."

"He probably deserved it." Said with great firmness. He pulled her around in front of him and studied her face.

"Don't you like my brother?"

"Not particularly. He's rude and I don't think he likes me. But then, I'm not sure you like me either."

"Well," he said, thinking over her perception of his brother and her insight into his feelings for her. "Look at the dogs," he said, mainly to get off this subject.

She did. The pair of them were still sitting, panting. John held out one hand. The dogs came to attention. His index finger bent. Both dogs dropped to their stomachs and waited for the next command.

"Bend down there and let them smell your fingers," he commanded. Emma, a little nervous, did so. First they sniffed her fingertips, then searched her hands. Finally the smaller of the two licked the hand.

All the tension was gone. Emma gradually moved closer and scratched each of the proffered sets of ears.

"You could have told me," she told him as she came up to her feet.

"Showing is better. Now, come over here." Looking away from him, she followed his lead. The dogs trailed along behind her. They went over to the cluster of oak trees that stood by the north corner of the house. Half a dozen saplings were spread in a circle some twenty feet in diameter. In the middle was a massively ancient trunk that vaulted skyward. A wooden seat had been constructed long years before around that massive trunk. It circled the tree, and used the trunk itself as the back of its seat.

"Relax," he suggested.

Emma nodded and smiled at him. She sat herself down very carefully. It was a seat for big men. Emma, big as she was, could just barely touch her feet to the ground. She sat at its front edge with her hands primly folded in her lap and said, "All right, now. Tell me."

"I'm trying to prepare a way to tell you what you need to know," said John. "We have a patient in a locked room. Maybe I said that wrong. Perhaps our patient has us. She may well be the owner of all this area and maybe we are, in fact, her servants. Or maybe she isn't the owner. That's one answer I'm still looking to the lawyers for. Interesting?''

''Well, who is it?'' Emma insisted, but she had a feeling of impending doom while waiting for his words.

He looked down at her and squeezed her hand gently. ''If you're really Emma Ballentine,'' he said, ''then I have a shock for you. The lady in the locked wing is your mother.''

Emma felt as if someone had hit her in the face with a pail of ice water. ''My mother?'' she asked, after she had taken a *big* gulp of air. ''That's impossible. My mother's dead. I——'' A sob was stuck in her throat. She struggled to clear it, and then whispered, ''I—don't know why I said that. Somebody told me, or I heard something, or—I just don't know. All I remember is my father and——''

''Please don't cry,'' John said rather imperiously. He had even said ''please.''

''I'll cry if I want,'' she snapped and tried to find her small lace handkerchief. She couldn't even find the pocket it was in. Her hands were shaking too much.

''Dear God,'' he muttered under his breath. He handed her one of his own massive handkerchiefs. ''One thing I can't stand is crying women.'' Then in a louder tone to Emma, ''What were you saying?''

''When?'' she sniffed.

''You didn't finish what you were about to say. 'And——' And what?''

Emma managed to regain her self-control. All her lonely life had been pointed toward independence, so her self-control was important to her. She refused to break down, again, in front of this man. Yet he asked as if he really wanted to know what she was thinking. Almost as if he cared.

"The only memory I have of the two of them is arguments. Loud voices. People screaming at each other. Someone throwing something that broke when it landed. I remember that sound of breaking glass, and to this day I cringe when I hear glass break. I wish I had the good memories that Jill has of her father. The last time my father spoke to me was after he hugged me at the social services center. He told me to be a good girl and then he kissed me." She swallowed hard; that memory had haunted her all her life. But she stiffened her spine and went on, "He came to my high school graduation. I told you that. He didn't speak to me. He just stood in the back of the auditorium. He looked out of place, that's why I noticed him. He looked shabby. But I recognized him."

"Was that the last time you saw him?"

"That was it." She paused, thinking back to that day. Then she continued, "You know, I'd always assumed my mother was dead. I never dreamed about her. I can't even picture her face. I find it hard to believe that she's— here." Emma started to get angry. For years she had suffered, believing that it was her fault that her mother didn't want her.

"What's she like? Where was she when I needed her? What did I do to make her not love me?" Then she heard herself. Heard the plaintive wail behind her words. Emma had always been a strong person. If she hadn't been, her childhood would have crushed her. This won't do, she thought. I can't cry over the past and I don't want to cry in front of him. The past is past. It's done. Nothing can change it. It's taken years for me to come to terms with life. Don't go backward. Get a grip, girl!

"I don't have any answers," John said. "Come upstairs and meet her."

"Now?" Emma said hesitantly.

"Why not now?" John replied. "Is there a better time?"

Emma shuddered. "She's ill?"

"She's got emphysema from a lifetime of relentless smoking. And cirrhosis of the liver from relentless drinking." He stood up, then reached for her hand. He towed her back into the house and up the stairs toward the locked door.

It's getting to be a habit, she thought, his towing me around as if he were a massive tugboat. But it was nice, and she wasn't going to complain—just yet, anyway.

"Emphysema? I thought they could cure that. Besides, if she's got it how can she scream? I thought it affected the lungs."

"Everybody is different, but it does affect the lungs. However, if she wants to scream, she'll find the breath." John was being very careful with his choice of words as they stood outside the locked door. Emma could tell he had fought for this objectivity. He hated the woman behind the locked door. Because she might be Emma's mother. If so, maybe he was prepared to hate her too? And I don't want that, she said to herself silently.

They could hear two voices inside the room. One was very excited and the other one very calm. When Nurse Snow finally came to the door, she said over her shoulder, "You have visitors, Mrs. Ballentine. Just look who has come to see you."

John leaned over and whispered to Harriet, "I hope this visit won't be a problem for you." Emma stared at him, and then walked by into the room.

"She's been excited since Jill came to visit," Nurse Snow assured him. "She's been talking nonstop about another visit. She really enjoyed the half hour with Jill. They ran me out of the room so they could talk privately. I hate to say it, but it looked to me as if they recognized each other."

Emma walked toward the back room of the suite. She could see a light and someone sitting at a make-up table with her back to the door.

"Come in, come in," the woman said as she continued to pat powder on her lined and sunken face.

"Hello," Emma said.

The woman at the table whirled and stared at her. "I don't know you," the woman whispered. A look of fear came to her eyes and she started to scream shrilly. "You're not Jill! Get out of *my* room. Get out of my life. I don't want to see you! I don't know you!"

CHAPTER THREE

EMMA was baffled. Why was this woman frightened of her?

"You're not Jill!" Mrs. Ballentine yelled. "Get out of here. I don't want you in my room. I don't want to see you." She had started out loudly and was now screaming hysterically.

Nurse Snow came bustling into the room as Emma tried to back out of the screaming woman's presence. "Get her out of here, John," Harriet said quickly.

John had followed the nurse into the bedroom and very quickly took Emma's hand to lead her out of the danger zone. By this time, in her hysteria, Mrs. Ballentine was throwing things. She threw a water glass that Nurse Snow had left on her bedside table. The glass hit the wall and smashed. Emma started to shake at the sound. She managed to hold up against the screaming and the fear she felt flowing from those faded eyes, but the shattering glass was Emma's undoing. By the time John had led her out the door, Emma was shaking so hard that one could hear her teeth chatter.

Behind them, from the locked room, came hoarse screaming that slowly softened and became inaudible.

"That was not exactly what I'd hoped for," John said softly as he took Emma into his arms. "What happened?"

"She thought I was Jill," Emma said between her chattering teeth. "When I spoke, she knew I wasn't and she started to scream. She didn't want me in her room.

46

I'm sorry, but if that's my mother—— Why is she afraid of me?" Slowly, Emma stopped shaking. "She said something when she first saw me, but I didn't hear it clearly." Emma twisted a little to get closer. It was so comfortable and warm in his arms. It would be nice if they could stay like this for a long time—perhaps forever? Wake up, Emma, wake up and smell the coffee. Your mother didn't expect you. Your mother? If she is your mother, he isn't going to want you. You can't be sure he even likes *you* without the handicap of your mother. Am I the wrong Emma? Is Jill her daughter? *Very* reluctantly, she pulled back from the warm cocoon of his arms.

Emma felt no embarrassment about having been in John's arms. It had felt like coming home. "Thank you," she said. "I needed that, and now I need to go to bed. It has been a *long* and *eventful* day. Good night. Will I see you tomorrow?"

"I'm here almost every day," John said. "I'm looking forward to seeing you tomorrow. You know where your room is from here?"

"I was at this door earlier," Emma replied. "I came when she screamed this afternoon. I can find my way to my bedroom."

"Listen," John said. "Don't take this all too much to heart."

"When my own mother disowns me like that? I need to take it very much to heart. Obviously I'm not the one she's waiting for. I think I'd better leave tomorrow."

"It may be," he said as he put his arm around her, "that she doesn't want to see you. But from where I was listening, Emma, I heard a woman with a very guilty conscience. Of course she wanted to see Jill. Jill is no threat to her."

"What do you mean by that."

"I don't have all the details yet. But think about this. Your mother is being expensively maintained in a nice comfortable cocoon here. One that she doesn't deserve."

"And she thinks I would push her out of her little nest? That's preposterous. Even if I had the power I wouldn't. She'd still be my mother!"

"You might know that, and I might know that," John said. "But, to a deeply disturbed mind like your mother's, anything could happen. Now, get to bed and get some sleep—and don't think about leaving here until after we hear the lawyers. Got that?"

"I—I've got that."

"Good night, then," John said as he gave her a little push in the right direction.

Emma opened the door and walked into the room she was beginning to think of as her own. She liked the place. The decorators had known what they were doing. The contrasting shades of green were comforting and relaxing. The more she saw, the better she liked it. It was—peaceful, and after a day like hers peace was welcome. She looked around for her nightgown and robe. If only I were better organized, she thought as she rooted through the drawers. If I were better organized I could just reach out and find everything I need. Oh, well! It adds spice to life. Now, who said that to me?

Just as she was trying to pin down the quotation, she heard a noise in the attached bathroom. It wasn't loud. It sounded whispery and—wet? Emma went to the closed door, knocked before she opened it. Jill sat on the side of the tub, crying.

"Can I help you?" Emma asked. "Is something wrong?"

"No," Jill said, "you can't help." She just barely managed to get the words out between sobs.

"Come on," Emma said as she sat down beside Jill and put an arm around the other girl's shoulders. "Come on. Just cry it all out. We're both orphans. What happened?"

"He hates me. He thinks I'm stupid," Jill whispered.

"Who?" Emma asked, getting angry. She knew that if someone was told often enough that they were stupid they gradually came to believe it. They accepted it. Growing up in foster homes had taught Emma that some people had a crushing need to dominate others. Sometimes they used violence and sometimes they used words. It was particularly bad on someone with little self-esteem, like Jill. "You're not stupid," Emma said softly. "Look at yourself. You're bright and charming. Don't believe everything you're told."

Jill didn't answer She kept on sobbing. She turned into Emma's body and laid her head on Emma's shoulder while she cried.

They sat there for about forty-five minutes while Jill gradually calmed down. By the time the sobbing faded away, Jill was half asleep and had to be helped into her own bed.

Emma returned to her own bedroom, changed into her nightgown, washed her face, brushed her teeth and climbed into bed. She must have been more tired than she had thought. She was asleep in minutes.

Emma was warm and comfortable, but something was trying to awaken her. She ducked her head under the pillow. Waking up was the most difficult thing she'd ever had to do. She was a night person. She did all her writing after midnight. But now, even hiding under the pillow didn't help. Warily she cracked open one eye. Nobody was in the room with her—nothing had changed. Except for the broad band of sunlight peering in through the uncurtained window, marked between sunlight and shadow by the waving branches of the maple tree outside.

"Somebody's trying to wake me up," she muttered disgustedly as she fought to untangle herself from the sheets. "Somebody. Signals. How lucky can I get?"

She fumbled her way to the window. The world outside was bright and clear. Had it been rainy she would have had no compunction about going back to bed, but bright sunshine? With one eye still closed, guiding herself along by trailing one hand along the wall, she finally found the bathroom and the shower.

Fifteen minutes later, with both eyes open, and her mind almost in gear, she dressed in her favorite outfit— a pair of jeans with a pink pullover blouse. She finished off the ensemble with a pair of pink running shoes. She liked this outfit. She wore it at home when she wrote. Today she wore it for the confidence it gave her. Yesterday had been an unsettling day; she needed the confidence. Besides, she was going to see John today. He'd said so, and that required more than a little confidence!

Emma made her bed. It was habit. She hated to get into an unmade bed and her foster homes had drummed the act into her. As she went into the hall the smell of coffee and newly baked bread took her prisoner and she followed the odors willingly. It was hard to believe that John had a brother like Luke. But then again, what did she know about families?

"There you are, now," Mrs. Macrae said as Emma came down off the last step. "You're up early. That's not a true Ballentine trait. Come in for breakfast."

Emma followed her into the kitchen. "None of the others is up this early," explained the housekeeper. "Usually it's just me baking the bread and maybe Mr. John if he's in the area. Now, what would you like for breakfast?"

"I'm not awake at this point, Mrs. Macrae." She grabbed in desperation at the coffee mug, and inhaled a few precious drops. "I'm not much for jump-starts. I like to slide into the day gradually."

"That's all right, my dear. Get used to the world before you make any decisions, including what you'll have for breakfast. I'll start some pancakes—in fact, I'll start some blueberry pancakes. Doesn't that sound grand?"

Emma was just finishing her second cup of coffee and second helping of blueberry pancakes when John stepped into the kitchen. It was just her luck that she had just taken an extra-big bite of breakfast so that she couldn't reply immediately to his good morning wish. He looked good enough to eat. Oh, not as tasty as the blueberry pancakes, but close.

"Good morning, Mr. John," Mrs. Macrae nearly carolled her welcome. "Here's your cup of coffee. Do you have some plans for Miss Emma today?"

"Yes," Emma murmured. "Do you have any plans for Miss Emma?"

"I heard that," John said as he leaned over her. And then in a normal tone, "I had planned to take her on a tour of Balleymore. Who knows? She might own the place."

Again that tremendous grin. Of course, Emma told herself, he's so big he has more face to grin with than most anybody I know. "Do you have a cup of coffee for Nurse Snow? I'll take it up to her now. I've got a message for her from Dr. Owens."

Mrs. Macrae gave him another cup, this one with cream and sugar for the nurse. He went out of the kitchen door to the staircase, whistling. Whistling? Emma asked herself. Is that a sign of early morning cheerfulness? Well, everybody is entitled to at least *one* fault. If his worst bad habit is early morning whistling, then I guess it's not too bad.

As she sat lost in thought, Mrs. Macrae stopped in front of her and held out a small pink polka-dot rag doll. "Here she is. You remember Gertrude, don't you? I made her for you when you were eight months old. She was your favorite doll. I found her in your bedroom after you left with your father. I couldn't believe that you'd forgotten to take her with you." The old lady's face was so bright with hope and remembrance that Emma didn't have the heart to tell her that the doll meant nothing to her. But it was something that the housekeeper had kept for years in memory of the little girl she loved. Emma would have loved to have a Mrs. Macrae in her memory, so she made an effort with the doll.

"Oh, so that's where Gertrude went," Emma said, hoping for forgiveness. "Imagine you keeping her all these years."

"It was all that I *could* keep of yours," Mrs. Macrae said. "After the two of you left, your mother cleaned everything out—except for Gertrude."

Be excited, Emma commanded herself. Show some enthusiasm. It's important! She reached out and took the doll carefully. It showed years of wear. By being treasured by Mrs. Macrae? She sat at the kitchen table cuddling the little thing against her cheek until John came down the stairs. When he came into the room she slid the doll into the pocket of her jeans. She didn't know why she did so, she just felt that she ought to.

"I'm certainly glad," John said as he entered the room, "that you dressed correctly for going out into the fields. I was afraid you'd be in high heels and short skirt."

"I should probably feel insulted," Emma said, grinning up at him. "But I've been stuffed with the world's finest pancakes and coffee and haven't any fight left. There's very little at this point that you could say that would insult me. So, as they say in the theater— lead on, Macduff!"

"Don't know the man," John said as he seized her hand and towed her away. A four-wheel-drive Jeep of indeterminate age squatted outside the front door. "Don't be put off by the car," he announced. "She works like a charm. I like her."

"With that as a recommendation," Emma said, "I have no fears or reservations. Where are we going first?"

John started the vehicle and moved it toward the driveway down the back side of the hill. "I thought you might like to see the east fields. They're the farthest from the house and the closest to my family's place. I've got some work being done there and I'd like to see how it's going. All the land we're passing through belongs to Balleymore. If you are indeed Emma Ballentine, this might all belong to you some day. Although I hope you're not expecting a large bank account to go with it. The estate was mortgaged heavily by Mr. Ballentine. For the most part, the farm is now self-sufficient, if not too many demands are made on it."

"How did you get involved in Balleymore?" Emma was curious.

"The estate had been managed by Mr. Jordan for a number of years but he died about ten years ago. The lawyers didn't know what to do so they just let it run itself. Unfortunately, it was running itself into the ground. About four years ago, the lawyers asked me to take over the management of the estate. I've been doing the job at their request until someone comes along to take over."

"Don't you like the job?"

"I like the job well enough, but——"

"But what?" Emma was curious about this man. She wanted to know him.

"As the conservator," John was slow to respond, "I'm not given much leeway. I'd like to make some changes. I'd like to improve the crop selection. I'd like to upgrade the machinery. But first, this isn't my property, and secondly, there's not enough money in the estate bank book to pay the mortgage payments and then improve too."

"You know," Emma said, "it has almost got to the point where I'm hoping that I'm not Emma Ballentine. Or, at least, your Emma Ballentine."

"Why is that?" John asked seriously.

"I've got enough money for myself," Emma replied, just as seriously. "I've got the money from the sales of my father's paintings and I make some on my own. I write. Did you know that?"

"I found that out," John said, "when I gave Mr. Hendricks, the family lawyer, your papers from New York. He's a big fan of yours. He loaned me a book last night."

"Which one?" Emma was curious.

"*Child of Rage*. I read it all last night. It's very good. I was caught up with the story. Were you writing about yourself?"

"Part of it was me," Emma said. "Other parts were other foster children I know. It's been peddled as fiction but the truth is that only the location is fictional. The characters are all real. But to keep myself from being sued I made minor changes in everybody except myself."

"Did you enjoy writing that book?" John wanted to know.

Emma took some time before she answered because she wanted to be precise about the answer. "I always enjoy writing at least part of each book. Sometimes it's the beginning, and other times it's some other part. Not every book I've ever written has been fun. That first book was *not* fun. It was too close to the truth. I've never told anyone that much about myself before. It hurt me and I was driven to finish it. I was working in Macy's in those days. Forty hours of standing behind a counter, and then every night at my typewriter. But when I was done I was proud of the result. It served as a catharsis." She squirmed around to see if he understood. He nodded.

As they were talking, they had come down the mountain to the lush green and flowering valley. It looked like the Garden of Eden, when Adam first set foot within. The road was lined with trees, and green fields spread on either side.

"All of this belongs to Balleymore? This is gorgeous! What is it that you farm around here?"

"We grow potatoes and apples. We have other crops, of course. And we rent out fields for local truck farmers. But our major crop is potatoes."

"So all of this other stuff is just for show?" Emma asked incredulously. "I've been out to Idaho and seen their potato fields. In fact, I wrote a book that took place in potato country. I've never seen such beautiful countryside. Isn't it a bit hilly? I thought tubers were a flat land crop?"

"The east fields," John informed her, "are as flat as any you'd see anywhere in New England. Flatness is a relative thing."

By lunchtime, Emma had finished viewing the fields. She now knew more about potatoes than she had ever thought she'd want to know. Every time someone came up to speak to them, she was sure they were about to tell her some more about the ubiquitous tuber. John was simultaneously overseeing the work being done and lecturing her on the care and harvesting of the potato. "I just thought you *grew* potatoes," she said, sighing. "Instead, you manufacture them. Right?"

"Right. Getting them to grow is only part of the problem. And for a farm this size the equipment we need runs into the millions." He took a look at her tired and perplexed face. "I suppose now that if you saw a potato you'd rather it be in a bag in the supermarket."

"You've got it," Emma murmured while trying to put a look of eager interest on her face.

"Come on," John said. He took her arm and led her back to the Jeep. "Let's go over to my house for lunch."

"The only question I have for you," Emma remarked, straight-faced, "is will we be having potatoes?"

"Only the fates can tell," he said, smiling.

The trip over to the Weld house was a fairly short one. They were pulling up in front of the large old-fashioned wooden farmhouse within five minutes.

"It's much newer than Balleymore," John said as he saw her inspecting the house. "In fact, nothing in this valley is as old as Balleymore."

"Why is that?" Emma asked. "I thought this valley was settled at the same time by a number of families."

John nodded and said, "Yes, there were a number of settlers who came out here to settle. But during the Indian uprising we call the King Philip's Wars, Balleymore, which was a wooden stockade at the time, was the only building left standing. Deerfield was burned to the ground and all the settlers were massacred."

"King Philip's Wars?" Emma repeated.

"The King Philip's Wars," John said in a history teacher's tone, "took place from 1675 to 1678. The local Indians were fighting not only the settlers but hostile bands from other tribes. This land was a prize piece of property even then. If I remember my facts correctly, two hundred and thirty settlers were killed and nearly two hundred houses and barns were burned. Balleymore was the only house left standing after the fighting was done. There's a lot of history in that house."

"I knew it was a historical monument. My detectives told me that it was."

"Detectives?" John spoke with suddenly aroused suspicion. "What detectives are you talking about?"

The question came so quickly that Emma was taken aback. "My father wrote me a letter before he died. I gave you that letter. He told me to go to Balleymore. I didn't know where or even what Balleymore was, so I hired a detective agency to find it for me."

"What did they tell you about it!" John asked fiercely. "Are you here for the developers? Did they promise you a fortune for Balleymore land? All that talk earlier, about having enough and not needing any more, was that all just to throw me off the track?"

"No," Emma snapped back at him. Her voice rose an octave, and her hands plucked at her blouse. "I just wanted to find myself. My father told me to come to

Balleymore. I have so many questions and no answers. Is it too much, to want to know who I am?"

"All right," John said, sighing. "I'm sorry, but I think I have the right to be suspicious. Suddenly, we have two Emma Ballentines who are both claimants to a very large property. And those developers would do anything to control this land."

"Well, don't look at me," she said huffily. "How would I know?"

He looked over at her, and the anger faded, superseded by a little smile.

The day had started off so *nicely* with the pancakes and Mrs. Macrae and the doll, Emma thought. Wait, she thought, "Gertie"? That's right. She reached into her pocket and brought the little doll out. The little pink polka-dot rag doll Mrs. Macrae had told her had been her best childhood friend. Something in her mind struggled to break out. Gertie? On the furthest periphery of her conscience there was a nagging thought. Something about a little girl, coiled up in a big bed, with only a tiny doll to cling to. She was whispering to herself, but John overheard.

"Who are you talking to?" he asked. "You do realize that talking to yourself is no way to prove anything?"

"Well," Emma said sarcastically. She was thinking about the little rag doll, trying to remember. And not succeeding. "Thank you very much for those kind words. I'll treasure your judgment all my life. Have you ever had a doll you loved?" She knew it was a silly question the moment it was asked. A huge outdoors man like John, and a little polka-dot doll?

Whatever else he was, John had a quick mind. "Somehow I get the impression that that doll is important to you," he commented gently. "Have you had it a long time?"

Honesty time. "I don't know, do I? Mrs. Macrae said—but I can't remember." And then a quick change of subject. "But that's enough about Gertie. I'm starving—is this your home?"

"This is it," John said as he brought the vehicle to a halt and climbed out. "This is the Weld farmhouse. My home. Welcome, Miss Ballentine." As he made the correct courtesies, John's brain was racing. She can't remember? If she were a fake there's no doubt in the world she'd be sure to remember. Honest as the day is long? This jigsaw puzzle was getting more confused by the minute! He wondered if he had all the pieces.

Emma scrambled out of the Jeep before John could come around and open the door. She smiled at him as she readjusted her clothing. "What a lovely welcome, Mr. Weld. I'm honored to be here."

She put her hand on his arm and they moved toward the front door. He smelled of after-shave and male perspiration. For some reason it was rather sexy, she thought. Come on, Emma, he's never going to be interested in you! You're too tall, too mean and you have red hair. Those were the things she had been teased about all during her childhood. The red hair came by birth; she had reached her present height at fourteen. Which meant she had towered over everybody she had known. She had long since told herself that height and red hair were not deformities, but a childhood of being the butt of jokes had taken its toll. She couldn't see any beauty in herself and she didn't think anyone else could either.

They reached the front door, which had a brass knocker and a rose wreath on it. John turned the handle and waved her in before him. They stepped into a small

entrance hall with another door in front of them. John
opened the second door and led her into the front room.
A wide circular carpet covered the floor, but in the dim
light its quality could not be measured. There was an air
of musty decadence about the place.

"I know it seems strange," John said, "but there's
nothing here that can harm you. Let's go to the dining
room. Maybe Mrs. Hitchens, my housekeeper, has lunch
on the table." He guided her to one of the left-hand
doors and opened it.

The room was large with a big old round wooden table
in its center. The table was surrounded with six ladder-
back chairs and was highly polished. At the head of the
table slumped a man who looked a great deal like Luke.
She could see the resemblance. He was blond, but with
gray in his hair and beard. While Luke looked streamlined and polished, this man looked stringy and scarred.
His face was so wrinkled it looked like a contour map.
His mouth was pinched as if he never smiled. It was a
petulant face, a sixty-year-old spoiled little boy.

"Who's this, then?" the man croaked. "Your fancy
woman?" He cackled maliciously at John. Then he
looked back at Emma. "I know you, girl. Where do I
know you from, eh?"

Emma was repelled by the man. Her fingernails bit
into the flesh of her palms as she tried to remain in
control. She said nothing. John must know him, she
thought; please let him take care of this.

"Hello, Father," John said with an edge to his voice
that Emma had never heard before. "You've started
early, haven't you?"

"Wouldn't you, if this was what you were reduced
to?" the old man said as he lifted his glass of amber-
colored liquid to his lips and drank the whole thing down.

"I should have better than this. I should still be in Paris! I deserve better!" He started to wave his glass around and it slipped from his hand.

Emma went over to pick it up and as she got close she could smell the alcohol. Another drunk, she thought. This neighborhood is loaded with them.

"Get me another drink, girl," the old man demanded drunkenly.

"No," John counterordered. "If you want to drink yourself into your grave, then you do it by yourself. Come on, Emma. Let's eat in the kitchen. The air is cleaner there." With that he guided her out of the dining room, still with a comforting arm around her, leaving the old man mumbling to himself.

They walked down the hallway to the kitchen. "I apologize for that scene," John said. "I didn't think he'd be up yet. He doesn't usually get out of bed until two o'clock in the afternoon. And he isn't drunk until three-thirty."

"It's all right," Emma reassured him, "I've seen worse. One of my foster parents was an alcoholic too."

"We all have crosses to bear, don't we?" John muttered, regaining his equanimity. "In a way, though, I'm glad you met him. I wondered if I should introduce you two. You have someone in common."

"Who's that?" Emma said, mystified.

"Your mother. Mrs. Ballentine." Emma could feel the cold in his voice as he mentioned her name.

Turning, with raised eyebrows, she questioned, "She of the locked room?"

"That's the one. She and my father ran away together to Paris years ago. It was the scandal of the decade— no, of the century, in this county. She ran away leaving a four-year-old daughter and her husband behind. He ran away from a wife and two sons. In any event, they lived on her money until he spent it all. And then, just to show you what a courtly old gentleman he was, when the money was gone he left her high and dry and ill in Paris. He just showed up here one morning at the breakfast table and expected his 'loving family' to forgive and forget his 'little' indiscretion. My mother never forgave him. She divorced him in short order and has now very happily remarried. I don't think I'll ever forgive him." That hard edge was back in his voice. When Emma looked up, it was to see a face set in stone.

"I'm sorry, but I don't have any memories of anything like that." After a moment, she asked, "If they spent all *her* money and he left her alone and broke in Paris, how did she get back here?"

"I went to Paris to get her. He never had money," John explained in hard, bitter tones. "He spent every cent of it there was. I had to buy the whole farm back from the mortgage holders. He gets a small allowance from me, which gives him enough to buy drinks and go golfing when he's sober enough to stand."

He had said that last statement in such a flat tone that Emma knew he hated his father almost as much as he hated the sick woman in the locked room at Balleymore.

"I don't understand. If you hated her so much, why did you go for her?" Emma said.

"I couldn't just leave her there," he said somberly. "My father boasted about it. He thought it was funny. She was expecting him to marry her, and instead he dumped her. Very funny. I couldn't live with my conscience if I didn't do something about it."

"Was she hard to find?"

"The French police laughed. They have more destitute people in Paris than you can dream of. Finding her was a matter of luck, not skill."

"Is that where she got emphysema?" Emma asked.

"She'd been picking it up all her life," John replied flatly. "She's smoked three to four packs a day for most of her life."

"So you retrieved her from Paris, and brought her back. You then stuffed her in a locked room. That was an improvement?"

"She's the one who specified the locked room," he returned. "She wanted to be sure my father never came near her again. I was happy to oblige. My father was responsible. For the sake of Balleymore and to clear my conscience I went looking for her. It was sheer luck that I found her."

"And now?"

"And now there are a million problems. She's dying. We think she may be the owner of Balleymore. She won't say whether she's made a will, and what's in it if she has. It's a terrible legal problem. So, even if you *are* Emma Ballentine, you might not inherit any of the family property. It all depends on that woman. The one who went into hysterics last night when she saw you."

Some hope, Emma told herself bleakly. Luckily I didn't want the property anyway. Or is that sour grapes? She reached out to touch his arm. At least that's something nice I've found, she told herself. John Weld is man enough to drive me to distraction, but most of the time it's a—comfort—to be around him!

CHAPTER FOUR

EMMA was up early the next morning. This time she followed her nose to the kitchen.

"Well, good morning." Mrs. Macrae greeted her with a big smile. "I see you can find your way to breakfast."

"I'm not totally awake, Mattie, but my nose is like a bloodhound's when it comes to fresh coffee."

"What did you call me?" Mrs. Macrae was stunned, yet had a happy look on her face.

"Mrs. Macrae. Didn't I?"

"I thought I heard you say 'Mattie,'" Mrs. Macrae said in a disbelieving voice. "Emma used to call me that when she was a little girl. She couldn't master the 'K' sound in my name, so she—what am I saying? *You* used to call me Mattie! I'd be delighted if you'd just keep on using that name. I knew you were you, Emma!" And then, after a second to reconsider, "That doesn't make much sense, does it?"

"Sense enough. I'd be honored to use that nickname, if you want me to. Even though I might not want to be Emma Ballentine of Balleymore." Emma had a serious look on her face as she looked straight into Mattie's eyes. She liked the housekeeper and she didn't want to hurt her. While she was waited for Mattie to respond she finished her first cup of coffee and reached over to fill the mug again.

"Emma Ballentine," Mattie admonished her, as if she could read Emma's mind, "I know that you're *my* Emma we've been looking for all these years. I knew my little baby when I saw you again. This is family land. The Ballentine family have been in these parts for generations. You have responsibilities, Ballentine responsibilities. Now, what do you want for breakfast?''

"What were you going to make for everybody else?" Emma didn't want to overburden Mattie. The housekeeper wasn't young any more. Her last statements to Emma had been fierce, demanding.

"I tell you what, I'll make you French toast. That was always one of your favorites."

"French toast is *still* one of my favorites. It sounds delicious." In an effort to appear unconcerned, Emma was very offhand about the next question. "Where's John? I thought he'd be here by now."

"John went off this morning to Boston to go to the flower market," Mattie replied as she vigorously whipped up the eggs and the milk, and set a piece of bread in the dish to soak.

"Why did he want to go to the flower market?"

"The Weld farm grows flowers for a cash crop," Mattie replied. "Didn't he show you his fields yesterday? They grow a lot of other crops, but flowers are what make the money. All sorts of flowers in season, but roses the whole year-round. In their hothouses, of course."

"We only had a peek at anything not Ballentine land yesterday," Emma said. "Oh, well."

"Well, now, I've got one serving of French toast done. Here you go, girl. Do you want some syrup?"

"I'd love some syrup," Emma responded. "Why don't you sit down with your breakfast coffee and talk to me while I eat?"

Mattie sat down willingly enough. This talk about not wanting to take over the Ballentine property and name had frightened her. She was more than willing to talk to Emma about what she knew of the family.

"Do you remember my father, Mattie?" Emma asked rather hesitantly. "And what happened when he took me away? I heard you say earlier that I could have stayed with you. What did you mean?"

"Your father," Mattie said with regret, "was a lovely man who inherited a farm and didn't want to be a farmer. He wanted to be an artist. He lived for art. Your mother was a model he'd fallen in love with. I'm not sure why she married him. She probably thought he had money. From the start they had problems. Part of the problem was that your mother was a better artist than he was. You were born nine months to the day of their marriage. I loved you from the beginning and you often came to me when things were rough. When you were three your mother met up with Mr. Weld, Senior. They had a widely talked about affair and she asked for a divorce. Your father gave her one, but he refused to give you up. He knew that she'd use you as a club to beat him with. Her price was half a million dollars. To get the money he mortgaged the estate to the hilt. That's why it's so in debt."

"If he'd paid her off——" Emma wanted to be very clear on this subject "—why did we leave and go to New York? We could have been together here. Not separated like in New York."

"Sweetheart," Mrs. Macrae continued, "he took you away because your mother threatened to kidnap you. He was afraid that she would do just that and then ransom you for more money. I offered to care for you, but he said that the fewer people who knew where you were, the safer you'd be."

She had just given Emma an entire lifetime of information and Emma was going to need a great deal of time to digest it.

"Now that you've finished your breakfast," Mattie said with love and considerable determination in her voice, "I'll make some more for Nurse Snow." She got up slowly from the table and Emma thought she looked tired and just a little worn.

"Why don't I take Nurse Snow's breakfast up to her?" Emma asked quickly.

"I'll be thanking you for your consideration. Those stairs seem to get longer every year. I was thinking that somebody had been adding steps, but I'm just getting old."

Emma took the stairs carefully. She was carrying a tray holding a small pot of coffee, a covered dish of French toast, a glass of orange juice, and various assorted cutlery. It required a nice sense of balance. When she got to the door, she knocked and waited.

Nurse Snow came to the door and when she saw Emma with her breakfast she smiled. "I wasn't sure when I could get down for breakfast. Thank you," she said. "I need the coffee. Mrs. Macrae's meals are not to be missed."

"That's what I think," Emma said. "I'm almost afraid that I'll eat myself into a size sixteen."

"I wouldn't worry about that," Nurse Snow laughed, looking her up and down. "Not yet, anyway."

Harriet took the tray and put it on the table in the corner of the room which served as the sitting room of the suite. From behind the closed door to the patient's bedroom she could hear the chatter of voices.

"Mrs. Ballentine," Harriet said as she saw Emma look at the door, "has a visitor this morning."

Just as she said this, the door opened. Jill stood in the doorway, looking into the sitting room at Emma and Nurse Snow. There was an expression on Jill's face that Emma had not seen before. She looked like the cat who had eaten the canary. All that was missing was a few feathers around the mouth. "Mrs. Ballentine wants to see you," she told Nurse Snow.

"Well, if that's the case, I'll be going back down," Emma said.

"No," Jill said. "Mrs. B. wants to see *you* in just a moment. Wait here. I'm just as glad I didn't have to go track you down."

Now, isn't that strange? Emma thought to herself as Harriet went into the patient's room. If she *is* Emma, why doesn't she call Mrs. Ballentine "Mother"?

Harriet came out of the room shaking her head. "I don't know why she's demanding ice water to take her medicine, but she is. Are you going to be all right? She wants to see you now. I'll be as fast as I can. You know, don't you, that I have to lock the door behind me?"

"I can handle it," Emma said. She smiled as Harriet Snow left the room. But as the big tumblers in the lock creaked shut Emma had second thoughts. Her first experience with Mrs. Ballentine had not been all that pleasant. The idea of being locked in with her—relative or no—was not too palatable. But, damn the torpedoes, full speed ahead. Someone had said that once. He deserved a fat lip, whoever he was.

"C'mon," Jill snapped as Emma stood there gathering her courage. "Snow is only going to be away for a short time. We've got something to say to you."

Emma walked into the inner room. Mrs. Ballentine was sitting in her wheelchair next to the desk. Jill walked over and sat in the chair next to Mrs. Ballentine. Neither of the women said anything for a moment or two. The silence made Emma uncomfortable.

"Y-yes?" Emma stammered. "Did you have something to tell me?"

"We have a deal for you," Mrs. Ballentine said, never looking Emma in the eye. Her voice was weak and strained, but determined. "Something better than you could get elsewhere."

"A deal?"

"Yes!" Mrs. Ballentine snapped. "We're offering you money to get off the Balleymore farm and leave the state. Go back to New York."

Emma cocked her head to one side as she considered. The pair of them looked like two thieves preparing to rob the church coffers. "How much money," she asked, "are we talking about?"

"Five hundred dollars," Mrs. Ballentine said firmly, as if it were some wild sum.

Emma almost choked on the statement. Ten years ago, five hundred dollars would have seemed like a fortune. Now, with her book royalties coming in regularly and her father's paintings selling well, it wasn't as impressive. Don't be hasty, she told herself. Perhaps there's something more behind all this than five hundred dollars?

"I'd want some time to think it over," Emma demurred. Why won't she look at me? she thought. Is this woman really my mother? "That's quite an offer. Why are you making it?"

"We're making this offer," Jill said in a condescending tone, "so that when the lawyer says *I'm* Emma Ballentine you won't be left out in the cold with nothing."

"That's charitable of you."

"Yeah, you might say so." Jill seemed eager for Emma to jump at the offer.

Why? Emma asked herself. Why is she so eager? "How were you planning to pay me?" She stalled the negotiations for time.

"A check!" Mrs. Ballentine stated.

"No, thank you," Emma said. "I've seen too many checks bounce. It's got to be cash." Emma had questions just pouring through her mind. What is happening here? Did they believe I'd jump at their offer? Where's John? I want him here. Whoever said women were the gentler sex was talking out of their hats. These two made the Terminator look like a pussycat.

"Cash!" Mrs. Ballentine screeched. "You'll either take a check or get nothing."

"Cash," Emma stated in the cool tone she had learned in foster care.

"Jill, how much money do you have on you? All I have is fifty dollars in the desk," Mrs. Ballentine crumpled and appealed to her fellow conspirator.

"All I have is twenty dollars," Jill said, and she sounded startled, "and it's in my purse in my bedroom. I thought you had the money!"

"Not here," Mrs. Ballentine said. "I have it. But not here."

The key rattled in the sitting room door, and Nurse Snow came through. Saved again, Emma told herself with a sigh.

"Well," Emma said, hastily, "here's Nurse Snow. I really must go. It's been a pleasure talking to you both."

Immediate hysteria broke out. The nurse took her time coming into the room.

"Well, let me make *you* an offer," Emma announced coolly. "I'll pay each of you a thousand dollars. For you just to go away, Jill, and for you—Mother—to accept me as I am. How's that for an offer?''

"Where would you get two thousand dollars?" Mrs. Ballentine demanded harshly.

"I've earned quite a bit of money with my writing and my father's paintings are selling well."

"How could you find anybody blind enough to buy one of your father's paintings? I'm a better artist than he ever was."

"You know," Emma said as she looked down at the seated pair, "you're the second person that's told me you were the better artist. But I've never seen any of your work for sale in the galleries."

Mrs. Ballentine made an effort to get up out of her chair, but only managed a halfway movement before she fell back into her chair. "Get out of here," she snapped. "Get out of here and don't come back!"

"Too bad you're not my mother," Emma said, sighing. "Because I'm the real Emma Ballentine. If you're not my mother, just who the devil are you?" There was a moment of surprised silence. And that's the best throwaway line of the day, Emma told herself as she spun on her heel and stalked out of the room.

"Trouble?" Nurse Snow asked as they passed each other.

"Not for me," Emma said flatly. "I'm sorry if it's more trouble for you, but I just couldn't hold back any longer!"

There was a slight wind blowing from the west. Emma pulled the pins from her hair and let it all blow out behind her. The bench at the oak tree was welcoming. She strolled down and seated herself on the bench and closed her eyes. The world of scents crowded in on her. The sounds of life, birds and cows and insect swarms and—yes, cars, filled her head.

A soft footstep rattled the pebbled walk. The bench settled just a slight bit to accommodate more weight. A masculine arm came around her shoulders, and a self-pitying tear stole down one cheek. "She knows I'm her daughter," she complained into the male chest. "I can see it in her eyes whenever we talk. But she won't admit it! Why, John?"

A little chuckle shook his frame and bounced her head from side to side. She opened one eye. It wasn't John. Emma struggled to move away from him, without success. Luke was too strong for her.

"Relax," he said, pulling her a little closer. "Misery loves company. Nobody around here is more miserable than me."

A fresh set of tears cut loose from Emma's eyes. She continued to struggle against him, but his arm was immovable. Eventually she gave up and relaxed.

"Whatever goes around comes around," he said. "Money is the name of the game. Why is it that I'm the second son? No, don't try to answer that. I'll tell you. John is the first-born. Just for that he got money from Grandfather Harris. It was enough for him to buy back the Weld farm. Grandfather Harris was a great believer in primogeniture. He got the works. I got diddly squat!"

"It's tough on you," Emma said, stifling her own tears. "But that's the way of it. Nobody ever promised you a rose garden."

"No, but at least I ought to get an even break. It can't be too long before my father goes. Lord, his liver must be pickled already. But then what? John already has the Weld farm, and here he is running Balleymore at the same time. Lucky? Sometimes I think it's more than luck. He's pushing to control the entire valley!''

"I don't think I understand," Emma said.

"Don't be a fool," Luke snorted. "He's angling to get his hands on Balleymore. He thinks that if either of you inherit then he can come in with an offer to buy the land. But I've let Jill in on the secret. There are developers waiting with money, more money than John has, to buy the same land. He knows that I've put Jill in on the know. I guess he's working on you so he can get the land cheap."

"Why does he want Balleymore?" Emma asked.

"Your mother ran off with our father," Luke said. "John holds your mother responsible for our parents getting a divorce. He hates all Ballentines and would love to see you all disappear. You weren't getting any romantic ideas about him, were you? He'd rather sleep with a viper. He's said so! I've heard him."

"So why are you telling me all this?" Emma asked.

"I don't want to see you get hurt over John. John uses women."

"Uses women?" Emma's instinct was to disbelieve this accusation.

"Yeah," Luke said angrily, letting his polished mask slip with envy. "He uses them to get ahead. My big brother doesn't need women for anything else. He's only out to get what he can from everybody."

Emma was too shocked to answer. She managed to squeeze out a little space between herself and Luke, enough space so that she could look up at him. He believed what he was saying. His face looked as if he was eating a lemon, with his mouth all puckered up and sucked in.

"What do you get out of all of this?" Emma asked with the suspicion of a New Yorker.

"I can be your agent," Luke said quickly, with the mask coming back on. "I know who the developers are and how to get hold of them. All I'd ask is a percentage of the selling price." He looked so disingenuous that Emma knew she didn't trust him. But the things he said about John all seemed to add up.

"I'll have to think it over," she told Luke.

"Good," he said rather heartily.

She managed to eke out another few inches between them. "I can't give you an honest answer," she said finally. "I don't know my own mind. When I make up my mind, I'll let you know. Fair enough?"

"Fair enough." He smiled at her; a broad all-knowing smile. His teeth looked like pure white ivory planks in a wall. John, she remembered, had one of his incisors just a little bit crooked. Did it make a difference?

He got up from the bench and pulled her up along with him. "I think we ought to seal this little pact with a kiss," he offered.

Emma was not exactly willing, but not unwilling either. There hadn't been a great deal of kissing going around in her life. His mouth came down on hers gently, sealing out the outside world. There was some sort of magic in his kiss. When he released her and stepped back a half-step she ducked her head so that he would not be staring into her eyes while she struggled to rearrange her world.

He leaned in her direction and used one finger to tilt her chin up. "So. Not exactly dynamite, Emma?"

She agreed.

"But not a failure either, right?"

She nodded again.

"Well, for a first step, I guess I can't complain," he said.

"But—what about Jill?" she stammered.

"Jill? She has to take her chances in the game, just like the rest of us." He turned and walked away.

A game? Was that all this was? Emma brushed back her hair and watched him stride proudly away. A game? If so, it was the most important game in the world, the game of love. And she didn't even know the rules.

John Weld did go to the flower market, and managed a reasonably large sale for Weld farm, but on the way back he detoured by way of Deerfield, and the law offices of Arthur Hendricks. The slight old man was pleased to see him. Almost eighty years old, Hendricks had removed himself from the active practice of law, and spent his time only on the cases of his old friends and their descendants.

"Balleymore," he mused. His eyes twinkled as he led the younger man back into his inner sanctum. "Yes, I remember Balleymore. Who wouldn't? The upper crust of the valley, the Ballentines. And the Welds as well. Remember them all too well, I do. But I haven't heard a word of gossip about them in the past few years. What can I do for you?"

"You would remember that when Mrs. Ballentine was brought home I was appointed conservator for her?"

"Yup. A narrow choice of words, son. You were appointed conservator for the estate, not for Emma Ballentine. Finest boondoggle I've heard of, that. So what's your question?"

"I'm afraid I don't understand the difference," John said as he slumped into the proffered chair. "Boston isn't all that far away, but driving down and back wears me out. The difference?''

"Suppose you ask your question first?''

"Well, I had a conference with Dr. Weston and Dr. Owens just yesterday. They tell me that Mrs. Ballentine can't possibly last too much longer. As conservator I need to be ready for that eventuality. I thought perhaps you might show me her will?''

"I don't know that I would,'' the old lawyer said. "Even if I had it. Which I don't.''

"You don't have Mrs. Ballentine's will?''

"I surely don't.''

"But I—I thought you handled all the family legal business?''

"I do. Or at least I used to.''

"My God, what am I going to do if she drops dead tomorrow?''

"Don't see why you should worry. But then the Welds always were worriers. No need of a will. She doesn't have anything to leave to anybody.''

"But there's the estate, which has the developers foaming at the mouth. That's worth a great deal of money.''

"I do have something that might make your job easier,'' the lawyer said. He got up and rattled his way over to the wall full of files. "Now let me see, did I file that under B? No, under D.'' He sneezed as dust rose from the file box. "D for divorce, eh?''

John shook his head. The old man, even at the time of the Ballentine divorce, had been slowly losing his cookies. But he was an expert at civil law. Mr. Hendricks dropped a bundle of papers in front of him. Dust rose again, and tickled John's nostrils.

"A Bill of Divorcement," John read, and then ruffled through the pages.

"There are too many 'whereases' for me to make this out," he complained after a moment.

"Sewed it up so tight nobody could break it," the lawyer retorted. "It's simple enough. At the time of the divorce, Mrs. Ballentine wanted cash on the barrelhead. To get the funds, Edward mortgaged the farm for every penny he could get. She took all the cash, he held on to all the property and the child. So when Mrs. Ballentine passes over, she won't need a will. She doesn't have a thing left to leave to anybody."

"Nothing?"

"Not a red penny. If I remember rightly, four hundred and ninety-five thousand dollars she took. Grabbed it and ran, she did. And, as I understand it, blew it all on fast living in Paris. With your pa, that was, wasn't it?"

"My God, almost half a million dollars? And yes, my father helped her to spend it. So who inherits?"

"All the property belongs to Mr. Ballentine——"

"Who is dead already," John interrupted.

"Well, that makes it easy," the old lawyer chuckled. "His heir inherits, lock, stock and barrel. Just the one little girl, wasn't there?"

"Yes, just the one little girl. Emma. She was named after her mother. I hope the name is the only thing the child ever got from her mother."

"If Mr. Ballentine is dead," the lawyer advised, "you'd better file his death certificate and let the courts hand over the estate to the girl. Must be in her twenties by now, I suspect. You know where she is?"

John scrambled to his feet. The lawyer was a short man; all his furniture was cut to his size. John fitted into it about as well as he could squeeze into a Volkswagen.

"As to that, Mr. Hendricks," he said, "yes, I know where she is, but the trouble is that there seems to be two of her, and I don't know which one is which!"

"That'll make a grand suit," the lawyer said, laughing. "What does the property go for these days?"

"Something on the order of four million. At least, that's the figure the county assessor's office uses to fix taxes."

"You'd better figure out some infallible test to get the right girl," the lawyer advised, "or the only ones to make a profit out of this will be the lawyers."

"I was hoping," John said, "that you would continue to represent the estate?"

"Might be fun. But I'm not as fast as I used to be. No, what you—what *we* need is a guaranteed test *before* we get to probate the father's will. Mr. Ballentine, he did leave a will, I suppose?"

"He did, if it's legal. A handwritten single sheet, leaving everything to his daughter. I sent the whole packet of papers down to you."

"I do remember," the old man said. "Haven't got around to it yet, but I will. I think the best thing you can do then is to leave all the matter with me. I'll fiddle around with it. With so much money involved, this will have to go to probate court, and there'll be an inheritance tax, you know. The Commonwealth of Massachusetts insists on getting its share before even the lawyers get theirs. You get along now, boy. I need a nap before supper."

It had been a long time since John Weld last had been ushered out onto the street, but this was done with a lot of *savoir-faire*. He found himself out on the pavement under a late summer sun, and nothing taken from the load of worry he had brought in with him. Still, it made for some interesting speculation. Mrs. Ballentine had already spent all *her* inheritance. Emma would collect the rest. And with that thought his heart fell through to his toes.

If Emma Ballentine inherited four million dollars' worth of property, would she be tempted by the developers' offer? She could very easily sell the land for an enormous profit. She'd also put twenty families employed on the estate out on the street. Would she care? Neither her mother nor father did; why should he expect her to be different? Would she wind up the whole estate and make her way back to New York and the publishing world? Why did he want her to be different from her parents? Why was it important to him that she be responsible and caring? I hate the Ballentines! I've got to keep reminding myself of that fact, he reiterated to himself. I can't lose sight of what they did to my mother.

Disgusted with a world where he could lose on both sides of the argument, John walked down the street to where he had parked his car, and started off for home. Halfway up the hill he stopped at his favorite place, a parking area and a lookout. There was a clear view to the top of the hill as well, where the old stone house stood. It was something he did often. Even before all this to-do about the two Emmas had come up, John Weld had been in love with Balleymore. Now, he suddenly realized, it meant something more than it ever had meant before, because Emma was a part of it.

There was a warmth, a sincerity to that woman. More than he had ever experienced before. Love? Well, hardly, I've only known the woman for a few days, he argued with himself. I'm not going to fall over backward just because she has a cute little chin. That's the way Luke might respond, but not me. Besides, she's a Ballentine. Just keep reminding yourself of that fact, he told himself.

He leaned back against the door of the car and scanned the house on the hill. There was a flash of white just back there by the oak tree. Grinning at his new voyeur status, John fished in the glove compartment of the car and brought out his field glasses. He cleaned off the lenses and brought the scene into focus. Emma it was, charming, loveable Emma. And his damned brother Luke kissing her. Jealousy ravaged his mind. He almost threw the glasses over the side of the road before he regained control.

"So that's the game," he muttered. "She's just like her mother. Make a play for the pretty one. Break up a relationship. She's trying to get between Luke and Jill just as her mother broke up our parents' marriage." Hold on a minute, he thought, you know that your father went willingly. Luke is probably very willing too. He probably thinks that Jill won't make the final cut and he's hedging his bets. He won't work for his wants, but he'll scheme for them. I wonder what story he's told her? On the other hand, she must be like her mother if she accepts his story. I was right! I got too caught upon her big green eyes and soft white skin. The Ballentine women are all poison!

Emma was still sitting out back, enjoying the mountain view, tracking as best she could the old Mohawk trail. It stretched about one hundred miles from Greenfield to North Adams in Massachusetts, and then over the crest of the mountains to Stillwater, New York, thus connecting the headwaters of the Connecticut River to those of the Hudson River. Most of her tracking was imaginary. The trail itself was a narrow highway that wandered through a myriad tree-covered lands, and only occasionally came out in the open for a solitary viewer to admire.

The back door of the old stone house opened and closed with a slam. Singing at the top of her lungs, Jill came out, located Emma by the oak trees, and came running.

"Oh, Emma," she called excitedly. "She did it! She really did it!"

Emma focused her eyes and leaned back. "Did she really? How wonderful!"

Jill came down to earth with a thump. "You don't even know what I'm talking about," the girl muttered.

"No, I guess I don't. But if it made you happy, that's all that counts."

"Emma Ballentine, don't treat me as if I'm stupid," Jill huffed. But then her excitement overcame her again. "Mrs.—my mother finally signed her will. Oh, I'm so glad."

"Ah. Might one inquire who gets what? If I'm not being too nosy?"

"Well." Jill plumped herself down on the sturdy wooden seat to compose herself. "You'll never guess!" An enticement to ask further questions. And Emma was not at all concerned about asking.

"No, I'm sure I'll never guess," she said. "Who? What?"

"Me!" Jill was up on her feet and danced around like a little girl with two ice creams for Sunday dinner. "Me," she repeated. "I'm to inherit everything."

"Well, isn't that nice?" Emma retorted. "Lock, stock and barrel. Nothing for Nurse Snow? Nothing for Mrs. Macrae?"

"Nothing." Jill danced one more circle around the trees, and then stopped before Emma with a solemn look on her face. "And oh, dear Emma—nothing for you as well."

"Not to worry," Emma told her. "I don't need the money. It might have been fun to live here with someone I loved, but that's the way the cookie crumbles. I congratulate you, Jill."

"Thanks," Jill said with the same canary smile she had been wearing earlier. Having said her piece, and victorious in her quest, Jill went away looking for Luke.

Well, Emma thought, what happens next? So far today I've had a bribe attempt, and a very clumsy one too. I've been approached by Luke with a business deal and then kissed by Luke, when, if I were being honest, I'd have preferred John. Jill will inherit and I suppose that means that "Mrs. B." isn't admitting to being my mother. Once again, I'm an orphan.

Emma had almost come to terms with being a ward of the state, but it was a hard and lonely life. She was tired of being alone. She wanted to have someone she could call her own. But the die was cast; she shrugged her shoulders. I'll pack tomorrow, she told herself.

As she sat there ruminating on the twists and turns of fate, John came striding angrily around the corner of the house.

"I was right," John said with a furious frown.

"Right about what?" Emma asked.

"You're just like your mother! You can't keep your hands off other women's men," he said with malice.

"What are you talking about?" Emma asked.

"I saw you up here kissing Luke. Just as I saw your mother kissing my father years ago. You're a real chip off the old block, aren't you?"

"Well," Emma said as she rose from the bench set. "If that is the general feeling, I guess I'll go and pack this afternoon. I can be on the road by dinnertime."

"You can't leave," John said. He sounded as if she'd taken all the air out of his sails.

"Why not?" she asked. "Jill has just come to tell me that she'll inherit everything because Mrs. Ballentine has signed a will naming her the beneficiary."

"What does she have to do with anything?" John looked confused and astonished.

"She just told me that Mrs. Ballentine has written a new will naming her as beneficiary of all that Mrs. Ballentine owns at her time of death. We're taking that to mean all the Ballentine land and fortunes."

"Mrs. Ballentine can write as many wills as she wants and it won't make any difference to the distribution of the estate," John snapped. "You can forget about all that."

Why is he so cold toward me? Emma asked herself. He acts as if he wants to bite my head off. Thank God I'm not in love with the man; he blows hot and cold so fast it makes my head spin.

"What do you mean?" she asked. "I was under the impression that the land and monies were Mrs. Ballentine's to leave to her daughter. I thought that her making a will said that Jill was her daughter."

"That last part may be so," John returned, "but Mrs. Ballentine doesn't have any property or money to leave to anyone. She got her share of the estate when she divorced Mr. Ballentine. She's broke. She is living here on the charity of the Ballentine name. And I cannot for the life of me believe that Jill is in any way related to any of this Ballentine branch! You can't leave."

With that said, John turned and walked stiffly to the back door of the house and went inside. Emma was left standing next to the tree feeling as if someone had just hit her. Stunned by his unexpected attack, she saw paradise slipping through her outstretched hands.

CHAPTER FIVE

IT WAS finally night and Emma retreated into her room.
She went upstairs just after dinner and tried to write.
Nothing came. She kept repeating in her mind the scene
in the garden with John. She replayed everything that
was said or done. Nothing changed.

Emma finally got up from the laptop computer. She
had been at the desk for two hours and accomplished
nothing. In disgust, she prepared for bed. She washed
her face and hands, brushed her teeth and got into her
blue-striped silk pyjamas. She was laughing at herself as
she put on the pyjamas. She traveled light. Two pairs
of blue-striped silk pyjamas, and two blue-striped night-
gowns. Having money gave her the joy of buying what
she wanted. But, having been raised in the tight budgets
of foster care, she wasn't an adventurous shopper.

She relaxed when in bed, but sleep eluded her. Her
eyes and body were ready for sleep but her brain was
wide-awake. What made John so angry? Was he angry
because I let Luke kiss me? How did he know, anyway?
He hadn't been up on the hill. Well, why *did* I let Luke
kiss me? What did I do? Emma's questions chased each
other through her brain and memory.

Like many foster children, Emma had believed that
her parents had left her because she had done something
wrong. She had been bad and was being punished. It
had taken her many years to overcome the belief. She'd
grown a shell which had made people think she was self-
sufficient. It was at times like these tonight that she knew

the self-sufficiency was only an appearance. "No," she told herself, "I can't blame myself for his attitude. It's not my fault." But she couldn't bring herself to believe her own argument.

What was it about John that was so appealing? I've met other men, she thought. Other men try to interest me. I've met better-looking men. Luke is better-looking. I've met Mr. Weld, their father—and I want no part of him. That could be Luke in forty years. Luke is already showing some of his father's more unpalatable habits. But the man is John's father too. Mr. Weld's face shows all the traces of drink and womanizing. If Luke is engaged to Jill, why is he trying to make up to me?

On the other hand, everything about John interested her. His strength, his consideration, his care, and his sense of responsibility, were traits that would carry him— and his family—through thick and thin. He worked at something and for something. He would make an excellent husband and father.

I've been looking for a man like John all my life, she thought. Now I've finally found him. Except that he hates me and my family. Evidently I don't know the full story. I want to be a part of his life—a big part. He seems to want me out of it entirely.

Before she could sink any lower into this morass of "I wish" the silence of the house was broken by a loud buzzer. It startled Emma so much that she jumped out of bed and reached for her robe purely on reflex. The buzzer was still going when she reached the hallway. It seemed to be coming from everywhere in the house. Lord, what was happening? Emma wished mightily that John were here, but he and Luke both slept at the Weld farm. Emma could imagine almost anything happening from the sound. She ran down the hall toward the staircase. There were noises from below.

Mrs. Macrae came puffing up the stairs. She was dressed in her nightgown, with an unmatched robe; her curls were covered with a floppy white nightcap.

"What's happening, Mattie?" Emma asked.

"That's the alarm Nurse Snow has." Mattie puffed while she looked through her bunch of keys. "She only uses it when she has an emergency and needs some help."

"Can I help?" Emma said.

Mrs. Macrae finally found the right key and unlocked the door to the suite. "Yes," she said as she quickly moved into the room, "we'll probably need all the help we can get. Come on, girl."

"Mrs. Mac," Nurse Snow called from the other room in the suite, "please hurry."

"We're coming!" Mrs. Macrae moved into the bedroom with Emma close behind her. "What do you want us to do?"

The room had changed since Emma had seen it this morning. All the medical equipment was out in the open and was in use—or Nurse Snow was *trying* to use it. She was attempting to get the tube from the oxygen tank into Mrs. Ballentine's nose. "She's too much for one person. Emma, see if you can hold her head still so I can give her this oxygen," Nurse Snow said. "She's having trouble breathing and needs it urgently. Whenever I get it on her face she fights it off."

Emma moved to the far side of the patient, who appeared to be unconscious but was tossing and turning. "Mrs. Ballentine, Mrs. Ballentine," Emma said softly. "Please rest easy. Nurse Snow has some oxygen for you. It will make you feel better. Please let her help you." As she talked Emma very gently took hold of Mrs.

Ballentine's head and held it steady. Suddenly, Mrs. Ballentine was quiet and still. Nurse Snow managed to get the oxygen tube to her patient's nostrils and the ghastly wheezing was partially stopped.

"Mrs. Mac," Nurse Snow said like a general overseeing the troops for a forthcoming battle, "you call the doctor. When you've talked to him, please come back. Use the phone in the sitting room." Mattie bustled out and just seconds later they could hear the sound of the phone being dialed. Emma brushed her mass of hair aside, and tightened her shabby robe. She looked across the bed at the nurse. Harriet Snow was as immaculate as ever, with her pressed white uniform and neat little cap. The comparison was too much for Emma. She shook her head disgustedly.

"What do you want me to do?" she asked. Her hands had gone from holding Mrs. Ballentine's head to gently stroking the sticklike arm.

"When Mrs. Mac comes back," Nurse Snow commanded, "I need to have someone call John and tell him we're having a crisis here. And see if you can get Jill to come and help. That would be useful." Harriet stood looking at her watch while taking the patient's pulse. There was a sad look on her face. "If she makes it through the night it will be a miracle," she murmured.

Mrs. Macrae came back into the room. "I talked to Dr. Owens' answering service. They'll beep him and he'll be here as soon as possible. I hate those pager things— I wanted to speak to the doctor himself. Oh, well."

"I'll go and call John," Emma murmured. She walked out into the sitting room and over to the desk where the phone sat. Next to the phone was a table clock. It was only ten o'clock; it seemed to be much later.

The phone was preprogrammed with the most used numbers. John's was the fifth and all Emma had to do was to push the proper button. The phone dialed itself and soon the line on the other end was ringing.

"Hello," John's deep voice replied.

"John, this is Emma Ballentine. Nurse Snow wants you to come over right away. Mrs. Ballentine is having a crisis. Can you come soon?"

"I'm on my way," John said. "Will you be all right?"

"Yes, thank you. Bye." Emma set the telephone back in its cradle. Yes, I'll be all right—just as soon as you come. And if that isn't love I'll eat a bullfrog!

She walked back to the other room. Both Mrs. Mac and Nurse Snow were busy. They appeared to have everything under control and were working like a well-oiled machine. Then Emma remembered Harriet asking her to get Jill in case they needed another set of hands. She turned on her heel and walked out of the door of the suite. It was ominous that for the first time the door was unlocked.

Emma knocked on Jill's door and got no response. She knew that Jill was in the bedroom because she had heard her come in earlier. Emma couldn't believe that *anyone* could be unaware that something was happening. That alarm was *loud*. She knocked and called Jill's name repeatedly. There was no answer. But there was a connecting door in the shared bathroom! As she walked through the connecting bathroom she could hear the sound of frightened sobbing. Emma tried the handle and it was unlocked. She opened the door.

"Jill. Are you all right? Mrs. Ballentine—your mother—is having a hard time right now. Will you come and help?"

"No. No," came a piteous wail from underneath the bedcovers. "She's dying! I know it. I won't sit by and watch somebody die! Besides, I'm stupid. I'd probably kill her trying to help. Tell them I'm not here, okay? Just leave me alone!"

"Jill, this is for your mother." Emma sat down on the edge of the bed and rested one hand on the girl's shoulder. "Won't you be with her for just a little while? It would mean so much to her."

"No, please don't ask me to go and watch her die. I can't stand it!" Jill was edging her way into hysteria. Emma got up to leave her behind in the dark room.

"All right," Emma said as she left the room, "I understand. You just stay here. I'll tell them something. You don't have to come."

As she walked back into the suite Nurse Snow looked up with all the signs of relief. "Will you sit with Mrs. Ballentine?"

"Of course."

"Thank you."

Emma sat next to the bed and heard the hissing of the oxygen and the labored breathing of the patient. She took Mrs. Ballentine's skeletal hand in her own and held it gently as her mind roiled. She could feel pity for the woman who might be her mother, and something else. Compassion? Or was it that same power she felt for John? Affection? Love? The old woman was trying to say something but her voice was so weak that the hiss of the oxygen tank was drowning out the words. She leaned closer and could just make out a disjointed statement.

"I'm sorry, baby. I'm really, really sorry." The semi-conscious woman kept repeating those two sentences over and over. "I'm sorry, baby!"

"It's all right, Mrs. Ballentine." Emma tried to re-assure the dying woman. "It's all right."

Time seemed to pass very slowly. Emma held the dying woman's hand. Gradually, Mrs. Ballentine calmed. The little circle of light around the bed became an island of tranquillity. Emma's mind slowly drifted away from the patient's difficulties to gnaw at her own trouble.

John. Why has he turned against me? What did I do? Why am I, Emma Ballentine, worrying about John Weld and what he thinks? I don't love him, she told herself firmly. Or do I? Friendship? Perhaps. But not love. I could hardly fall in love so quickly. Could I?

A noise in the outer room brought Emma back to re-ality. The doctor walked into the room and preempted her seat by the patient. At least, she presumed he was the doctor. He had all the personality traits of a auto-cratic small-town doctor. He was dressed rather badly, in a baggy old brown suit with cigar ashes on his yellow tie. Emma was willing, however, to give him the benefit of the doubt. It was late at night. Emma's watch read ten forty-five. The doctor was here. He could take over caring for Mrs. Ballentine. It was his job, wasn't it?

"All right, Nurse Snow," the doctor said while looking at the chart Nurse Snow had prepared. "Everybody out. Thank you all for your help. Now let Harriet and me do our jobs."

Emma stood up when the doctor entered the room and she was ushered out of the patient's room. Out in the sitting room Mrs. Macrae sat on the settee. John stood by the unlocked door. He looked exactly as she thought he would. His clothes were just thrown on and he was unshaven. Emma knew she had become entirely unwound. He could hardly ever look worse—and I don't care. I just—— No more debate about who loved whom.

She walked unsteadily across the room into John's arms. She couldn't remember how she got there, but this was no time to quibble. It was a safe haven. He would protect her. She didn't have to worry. John was here. He was holding her. She was safe. The tears came. She didn't know why. That woman in there is my mother, Emma told herself firmly. It's time to stop waffling. She's never been a part of my life but I'm not just a member of the audience. She's my mother. No matter what she's done, I can't help crying for her.

Suppose it was me lying there, all alone. Who would cry for me? Who would mourn for me? She cried for the woman next door, who might, this very night, be going to stand before her Maker. And then she cried for herself.

"Hey," John said as he held her close. "Cry all you want to."

The three of them, Mrs. Macrae, Emma and John, sat in the kitchen yawning and silent. They all looked like escapees from a sleep-deprivation laboratory. Mrs. Macrae and Emma were in their nightclothes. Mattie still had her little nightcap on. John looked more rumpled than he had at first, and his chin looked as if it was covered with steel wool. Sunrise was still several hours away. The chiming clock in the hallway sounded three and on its last note the doctor came into the kitchen.

John gave the doctor an inquiring look; the doctor shook his head. "I'm sorry, but there's nothing I can do for her," Dr. Owens said. "She's calling for Emma." He looked at Emma.

Everything in her rebeled against this call. "It's not me she wants. She wants Jill."

"No," the doctor said quietly. "She is very specific. She wants to talk to you. Please go up to her."

Wearily Emma got to her feet. She could see out of the window in the kitchen that the moon was making a pitiful attempt at peering through the gathered clouds. The night-lights in their wall sconces, dim though they were, painted the staircase in bright colors. She tried to put some order in her hair as she climbed the stairs. The doctor followed her.

"Come in, Emma," Nurse Snow said quietly. "She's still asking for you."

Emma sighed. She followed the nurse to the bedroom. Mrs. Edward Ballentine—Mom, Emma thought as she looked at the woman in the bed. Mrs. Ballentine looked almost like a mummy. Her face was fallen in and the oxygen tube lay across her face. She was still breathing. It was the labored intake of a struggling patient. Her eyes were open. She was trying to say something.

Emma dropped into the padded chair that the nurse provided. "I'm here—Mother."

One of the thin arms reached out. Emma caught the hand before it fell back on to the bed. Her fingers were squeezed. Not strongly, but with enough pressure to let her know that the response was real. The voice sputtered, for only an instant clear enough to be heard. "Emma?"

"Yes—Mother. I'm here."

The woman's voice became stronger, clearer. "Where's Edward?"

"I——" Caught unaware, Emma fumbled for something to say. "He's in New York, Mother."

"But you're here." A pause to master the oxygen intake. "I've been a fool, little Emma. Edward and I both."

"It's all past," Emma murmured. The stick figure in the bed stirred.

"We were both too weak, Edward and I. And jealous. How can you be jealous of your own husband?"

"It's not important now, Mother."

"Oh, it's important. We fought each other and neglected you. I thought that the rainbow life would never end. What a fool I was."

"None of us is perfect."

"No, but I've been less perfect than most. And you know what I found out in Paris, after the money was gone?"

"No. What?"

"I found out that I loved your father. Do you suppose he——?"

"I think he always loved you, Mother."

The woman in the bed sighed, a form-racking sigh that shook the bed.

"And you, Emma. Can you—forgive?"

"Of course, Mother. Everything is forgiven."

"That fool doctor says I'm dying."

"Even doctors make mistakes."

"Not this time. I want to be buried by Edward. Promise?"

It was a task filled with almost insurmountable problems. Her father was buried in Potter's Field, back in New York. Shall I tell her that? No, too cruel. "Yes, Mother. I promise."

"We shouldn't have married, Edward and I. We were both too weak to do what was right. I wanted excitement. He wanted to be an artist. It killed him that I was better at it than he was."

"It doesn't matter now." Tears were creeping out from Emma's green eyes, and streaking her cheeks. The dying woman closed her eyes and then opened them again, but only for a second. "Love," Mrs. Ballentine whispered. "I did it all for love. I left both of you for love and a pretty face. God, what a fool I was!"

"Love," Emma repeated. The woman who might be her mother closed her eyes. Emma was unable to disengage her hand. She settled down in the chair, prepared for a long wait. The room turned cold. Emma shivered.

Nurse Snow came in with a blanket and spread it over Emma's shoulders. The warmth was welcome. Emma flashed a thankful smile, and returned to her watch in the night. Time seemed to drag. Her shoulders ached; her hand, clutched by her mother, was slowly losing circulation. Her mother managed to get her eyes open again for a moment, and then she turned her head away. The sound of difficult breathing dominated the room. Emma leaned forward to rest her elbow on the bed. "She *is* my mother," she told herself fiercely. "She *is* my mother."

The nurse cleared her throat behind Emma's chair. The sound of the labored breathing had stopped. Emma turned her head to look. Her stiff neck rebeled. The nurse was checking for a pulse. She looked regretfully at Emma. "She's gone." The nurse leaned down to help Emma disengage her hand. The doctor came in to certify the death.

The clock in the sitting room struck. Three—four—five! Five o'clock in the morning. Life had ebbed in the predawn.

Emma struggled to her feet and went slowly to the door. I searched for a mother or father, she thought, for most of my life. Then, when I found them, they died. I have a right to cry. She was my mother!

Emma leaned back on to the frame of the door. The tears welled, rose and swelled. Her mother was dead, and Emma Ballentine was the only one to mourn.

She walked downstairs and back into the kitchen. John and Mrs. Macrae looked up as she came in. "She's gone," Emma said softly.

"Oh, my dear." Mattie got up and hugged Emma close. "I'm so sorry."

"I never really knew her," Emma said. "I could have loved her."

"That's all right, love," Mattie said comfortingly.

The doctor came in and said, "I've called the undertaker's. When they get here, they'll take the body and prepare it for burial. Can I have a cup of coffee, Edna?"

"Oh." Mrs. Macrae jumped up. "I'll be getting some coffee on right away. Do you want some breakfast as well?"

"That would be lovely." Dr. Owens looked at John and said, "You need to get in touch with the lawyers. I'll certify the death certificate."

"I'll do it first thing in the morning," John said.

"What was the cause of death?" Emma asked.

"It could be any number of problems that caused death. Or a combination of several of them. I'm saying the cause of death was heart failure. That's true. Her heart did give out. With all of her problems it may be a miracle that she lasted as long as she did."

"Do any of the rest of you want breakfast?" Mattie asked. "I'm making scrambled eggs."

"Yes," Emma said. "Scrambled eggs would be wonderful, Mattie. Can I help with something?" She looked down at the two pale hands, hands that had held her mother. "I've got to keep busy," she murmured. "I've got to."

"If you want," Mrs. Macrae said, "you can make another jug of orange juice. If you could do that and give the doctor a glass, it would be a great help."

Emma moved slowly, like a robot. If she kept busy she had less time to think. She felt terrible. Her mouth was fuzzy. Morning mouth, she had come to think of it. She needed a toothbrush and a wet facecloth. Or a dozen things to do, to keep her hands busy.

The coffee was ready and the eggs cooking on the stove when Dr. Owens came back into the kitchen. Behind him came Jill, looking sheepish.

"I'm sorry, everybody," Jill said. "I couldn't help it. I can't stand death. I couldn't help anyone."

"Don't worry," Emma assured her. "We were thrown out by the professionals in short order. Do you want some coffee and scrambled eggs?"

"Just coffee, please."

"And don't forget me," Dr. Owens said as he reached for the toast Mrs. Macrae had put on the table. "Orange juice is fine. But coffee is my life's blood!"

Emma turned to get mugs for the coffee and to put some more homemade bread in the toaster. As she turned, she almost ran into John. "Can I get you some coffee? Or perhaps some orange juice?"

"I'll get my own," he said. "I'm already up and I've got my mug."

Emma stared at him, studying the play of muscles in his face. They were back to a standoff. The moment of comfort in the locked suite had ended. She watched him as he poured his own coffee.

Her eyes followed him as he went over to sit at the table with the others. Emma found more mugs and poured more coffee.

"Well," Dr. Owens said after his first mouthful, "I'm getting too old for this kind of night."

"We're all getting older by the minute," Mrs. Macrae said. As Emma watched the elderly pair they exchanged a significant look.

Dr. Owens smiled but Emma could see a certain amount of sadness in his eyes. He was a good doctor, she was sure of it. He hated to see death and illness win at any time.

Jill left the kitchen quietly carrying her coffee cup. Mrs. Macrae joined Emma, John and Dr. Owens at the kitchen table and the four of them sat and finished their coffee.

"Should I make another pot, do you think?" Mrs. Macrae asked Emma.

"It probably wouldn't hurt to have at least half a pot on hand," Emma said. She was sitting in profile to Dr. Owens and suddenly she felt him looking at her. She turned her head to face him and saw an almost quizzical look on his face. It was the look that said I know you— but from where escapes me. He noticed her looking at him and he smiled.

"I'm sorry, my dear," he said. "It's been too busy for anyone to get around to introductions but I'm Dr. Owens. And you are——?"

"Oh, my!" Mrs. Macrae exclaimed. "This is my little Emma come back to Balleymore. You remember her, don't you?"

"It's been years, Edna," the doctor said. "But she does have the family look about her."

That phrase set Mrs. Macrae off on her hobbyhorse about the Ballentines and their bloodlines. The doctor evidently had been living in the area for a long time and knew many of the people Mrs. Macrae was talking about.

They were having a conversation about the change in generations. It was a conversation you could have heard anywhere in the world with the older generation wondering what was happening to the younger.

Emma found the whole atmosphere almost tranquillizing. She was beginning to faze out when someone knocked on the front door. John got up to answer the door. Dr. Owens stood at the knock and looked at the door of the kitchen. He was waiting.

They could hear John talking to someone at the front door. "It's the medical examiner's people," John said as he stuck his head in the door.

"Yes," Dr. Owens said. "They need to see me before anything else happens." He walked out of the kitchen and went to talk with the officials.

Emma was still partially in a daze. She viewed the proceedings as if from a great distance. Was she really my mother? she asked herself. And answered herself firmly. Two things are true. She was my mother, and I love John.

"Do you have some more coffee made?" John asked from the hall.

"You have a choice. You can take the last of the pot or you can wait for a new one," said Mrs. Macrae.

"I'll take the last cup," John said somberly as he came in, "and the first of the new."

Emma sat in the corner of the kitchen and John didn't see her immediately. When he *did* see her, the smile left his face. She had often heard the phrase. She had even used it in a book, but she had never seen a face of granite before. His face looked carved in stone. She extended a tired smile in his direction hoping that he would revert to the laughing companion she had come to know. There was no change. No matter how much she wished. She shrugged her shoulders and turned away. She was too tired.

Before anyone else could move Luke came sauntering into the kitchen. He was dressed to the nines with his patently new beige suit, his silk shirt, and his four-in-hand tie. He had evidently been out all night. He had the exuberance of too many drinks.

"Hello, everybody! I'll take a cup of coffee. Two sugars and milk. I was just passing by when I saw the lights." His eyes darted around the room and finally he spied Emma huddled in the corner chair at the table. "Well, there you are, good-looking," he said as he swaggered over to her. "Why don't we go for a roll around the countryside? It's deadly dull here. I can show you some excitement. Just go upstairs and get dressed. If you have difficulties with that, I can help. I'm very good at clothes."

The scene was like a stop-action film. Nobody moved. They were frozen in time. Suddenly, John exploded like a grizzly bear in heat. "Get away from her!" He grabbed his younger brother by the collar of his coat. "Outside," he commanded.

"Jealous," Luke sneered. "Jealous because she likes me more than you? God knows any woman would prefer a good-looking man over a bear."

Their voices faded as they went outside. There came a thud, and quiet. Moments later John returned alone, holding his right hand up in front of him. The knuckles were scraped. "Luke won't be back," he said, and returned to his coffee mug.

Would I prefer a good-looking man over the bear? Emma asked herself. I'd be a fool if I did.

She was tired. She finally got up the energy to get up from the table and say good-night or good morning to

Mattie. She kissed Mattie's cheek and trudged up the staircase to bed.

Jill was waiting for her. As soon as Emma went into the bathroom to find her toothbrush, Jill came through the connecting door. "Can we talk?" The girl's fingers were twining with each other. Her pout had disappeared, leaving her face drawn and pale.

"Of course." Emma was exhausted. But courtesy had always been one of her strong points. She would be courteous to the devil, if necessary. "Just let me brush my teeth and wash my face."

"I hate death," Jill said, sighing. "I'm a coward and I don't want to watch. I don't want anyone to think badly of me because I wouldn't help. Do you think badly of me?"

"There was nothing you could have done. Please don't worry."

"I have things to do," Jill said and she walked through the connecting bathroom to her own room. She closed and locked the door after herself.

Finally alone. Emma managed a long strained sigh. Her head hurt. Her bed summoned her. Before she laid herself down she was drawn to do something she had not done since she was a small child. She knelt down beside the bed and prayed for the woman who had just died.

CHAPTER SIX

THE house was still quiet when Emma came downstairs. The clock was chiming nine. Emma was still tired, but she couldn't sleep any more. She was going to have to look into curtains for her bedroom. She started a new pot of coffee and as it brewed she sat down at the kitchen table.

Her brain was stumbling over both the death she had witnessed last night and the anger John showed her. She was tired. She had found her mother and lost her. She had found the man she'd dreamed of, and then lost him. She knew life wasn't designed to be fair, having suffered through her share of unhappiness. Her whole childhood had been spent searching for someone to call her own. But then her father's letter had sent her to Balleymore. Balleymore equated with "home," and John was there.

A strong man, a good man, just the kind of man a woman could count on. Now, the courts might say that Balleymore wasn't hers and John—Lord, he might already have decided against her. Couldn't she win— just once?

She was pouring her second cup of coffee when Mattie came stumbling into the room. "What a night!" the housekeeper said as she poured herself a cup. Clutching her mug of coffee in both hands, she came to join Emma. "Last night was exhausting," she went on. "I didn't get to bed until the house was cleared. Oh, about six in the morning. How about you?"

"About the same. I bet it's the coffee smell that brings people down."

John proved the point. He came into the kitchen and went immediately to the pot, picking up a mug on the way. He filled his cup and came to sit with the ladies.

"There are things that have to be decided," he said.

"What things?" Emma asked cautiously.

"The funeral," he answered. "Just for starters."

"What?" Emma said confusedly. "Decide what?"

"Someone," John started very slowly and carefully, "has to decide where and when the funeral service is to be held and where she is going to be buried."

"Does the conservator do that?" Emma asked hopefully.

"No," he said. "A member of the family should do that. You were her daughter. It's your job. But I'll be with you if you need help."

Emma took a deep breath and relaxed. He would help? In that case it could be done.

"She told me," Emma mused, "that she wanted to be buried by my father. He's buried in Potter's Field in New York. I gave my word she would. How do I do that?"

"We can arrange to have his body brought up here and buried next to her." John was very definite on the subject. All Emma wanted to do at this moment was to leave everything in his capable hands. That aura of command that surrounded him soothed and calmed her. It was one of the things she was attracted to about him.

"When do you want to start?"

"Let me," Emma said, "take a shower and get into some clothes before I have to make any decisions. Okay?"

"Be my guest," John said with a return of the coldness he had shown to her earlier this morning. It was as if he suddenly remembered he didn't like her.

"Before I go," Emma said, "what did I do that makes you so angry at me?" She was just tired enough to be blunt with her question.

"I was under the impression," John said very precisely, "that you knew Luke and Jill were engaged."

"What?" Emma said stupefied. "Of course I knew."

"Then what," he said, standing, "were you doing kissing Jill's fiancé yesterday afternoon down by the big tree?"

Jealousy? Was that what this was? Emma was almost overcome with hope. But then—how dared he judge her so quickly without even hearing her side of the event? "Where were you when you saw all this?" she asked through clenched teeth.

"At the scenic lookout in the valley," he said self-righteously.

"My," Emma said after she pictured the overlook in her mind. "You certainly have *good* eyesight."

"I have a pair of fine binoculars in my car," John said with injured dignity.

"And with your binoculars," Emma said, "could you tell who was kissing and who was being kissed?" She stopped for a second. The anger was growing within her and was about to explode. "Your brother was kissing me. You may have noticed he is almost as large as you are. There were not many ways I could have got away from him!" She stopped for breath, and then returned to the war. "And you condemned me on what you saw without even asking me about it!" On that note, Emma whirled around to leave the room. John grabbed her arm to prevent her from leaving.

"If that were the case," John said, "then I must apologize. Please forgive me." The tone used for the apology was about as warm as spring water running down a mountainside. Mrs. Macrae, who had been hanging on every word, shivered conspicuously.

"What a deep and heartwarming apology," Emma said from between clenched teeth. "Listen, because I don't intend to repeat myself. Your brother kissed me. I didn't mind but I'm not going to make a habit of it. The idea was all his. You must know what kind of man he is. He tries to charm his way through life." By this time, Emma was almost shouting. "But *please* believe me, I didn't ask him to kiss me!"

John let go of her arm and she ran to the door. "I don't think I really like you, Mr. John Weld. You, your brother or your father," she yelled as she slammed the door behind her.

"Good Lord," John said. "What have I done?"

"Do you want a list," Mrs. Macrae inquired sarcastically, "or are you satisfied knowing that you've managed to insult a fine woman? One who obviously cares more than a little bit about you."

"You really think that, Mrs. Mac?"

"Men," the housekeeper snapped.

"But——"

"You're a fine farmer, John. Too bad you never studied anything else. Did you ever stop to tell her how you felt about her?"

"I—I don't even like her. She's a Ballentine through and through, and you know I don't like Ballentines. Besides, we've only known each other for——"

"Well, if I were you," the old lady said as she pushed away from the table, "I'd make up my mind just a mite faster! You can't hate the girl for the mistakes her parents made. That makes no sense! She's a lovely girl, Mr. John, and I think of her as mine. If you hurt *my* little Emma again, then I'll have words with you!''

Emma made it upstairs and rushed into the bathroom hiccuping after her bout of tears. She could hear Jill on the other side of the connecting door. Jill was still crying, but softly now.

Emma went into the bathroom and turned on the shower, dropping her pyjamas in a heap. The water was warm. She turned her back to the shower and relaxed. And then she thought about—what else? John. She was trying to cleanse her memories as well as her body. John attracted her, but it took two to tango, she told herself. There was no future with someone who would judge and condemn you in one fell swoop. In addition, to slanting events against you because of something our mother did many years ago. A one-sided romance meant heartache for somebody, and it didn't take much reasoning to discover who that somebody would be. Her daydream included roses and a white wedding. She came out of her dream with a grim laugh. Just keep your chin up, Emma—that way you're open for an upper cut to the jaw!

Moments later she stood in the bedroom all clean, dry and powdered, looking at her wardrobe. What did one wear to see a minister about a funeral? She decided on the most drab piece of clothing she owned. A brown shirtdress worn without the usual accompanying bright orange, yellow and green print scarf. She dug out her brown flats and put them on. She wore a small gold cross on a simple gold chain, a pair of small gold hoops in her ears and her birthstone ring, all gifts from herself to herself. "Okay, Emma," she said to her reflection in the mirror, "let's go. We're ready for anything." She crossed her fingers because she wasn't *that* sure.

John was waiting for her at the foot of the stairs. As she came down he ran his eyes up and down her body, as if he was inspecting her for defects. Her temper control began that long, slow rise toward explosion. She maintained control by biting on her lower lip.

"Is this all right?" she said about three-quarters of the way down the stairs. He winced, as if he were being stabbed by the sarcasm.

"Yes," he said, "you look fine."

"Good," she said with a self-mocking smile. "I've never had to organize a funeral before. I wasn't sure what would be correct."

"Didn't you do it for your father?" John asked.

"No," Emma replied. "I didn't find out about his death until several weeks later. They buried him before they found me. All I got to do was go and clear out his rented rooms." She could feel her eyelashes tangle themselves in the tears. Suddenly there was the softness of a handkerchief on her face, catching the drip. "Thank you," she said in a voice muffled by the handkerchief. "I don't normally dissolve into tears and I'm not sure why I'm doing it now."

"It's all right," John said softly. "Someone should cry for both of them. If you don't, who will?"

"Well," Emma said bracingly, "let's get going."

John drove skillfully. The sun was just rising over the eastern hills, but life in the country village was already stirring. "Saint Stephen's United Methodist Church is the Ballentine family church. I'm fairly sure the Ballentines have a family plot in the cemetery," he said.

"Oh, boy!" Emma said with a hint of despair in her voice.

"I know this isn't easy," John reassured her, "but it has to be done. The minister is wonderful. So don't worry about it. Besides, I'll be here with you."

It was this last sentence that reassured Emma more than anything else. If John was going to be there, she would have support. Even if he thought she was a tramp. It was the same feeling one could get with a torn life-jacket. There was a chance of sinking and a chance of learning to swim very quickly. Either way, it was a comfort, if you didn't look too closely.

It was a short drive to the church. As John looked for a parking space Emma got a good look at Saint Stephen's. The building was half brick and half wood. The plate in the corner stone mentioned 1802. Which must have been a good year for Methodist churches, Emma told herself almost hysterically. In the neighborhood where she had last lived nothing was over twenty-five years old, and part of that was falling down. This building was in excellent condition. She could see a figure walking across the well-kept grounds toward a side door.

Before she could comment, John said, "Good, there's Reverend Hardy." He honked his horn as he got out of the Jeep and the figure turned to face them.

Reverend Hardy was a tall, thin woman with gray hair and a pair of sparkling intelligent eyes. The reverend was dressed in an old pair of yellow pants with a faded blue T-shirt that once had some design on it.

"Hello, John," the reverend said. She had one of the most beautiful speaking voices Emma had ever heard. She could envisage people paying money to listen to this woman read from the phone book.

"Reverend Hardy," John started the introduction, "this is Emma Ballentine." The two women nodded.

"Mrs. Ballentine died last night and we need to arrange the funeral services."

"I'm so sorry," Reverend Hardy said. "Had I known earlier I would have paid a sympathy call. My name is Barbara and I would be pleased if you'd use it. Come into my office and we can set up a date."

Barbara Hardy led them to the side door. Her office was on the first floor behind the sanctuary. A secretary sat in the outer office, typing madly at a word processor.

The minister sat down at her desk and picked up a book from the shelf behind her. "It seems to me that the Ballentines have a fairly large part of the cemetery, with plenty of plots left." She ran her finger down a column in the book. "Ah, yes, here it is. Do you wish to bury your mother in one of the family plots?"

"Yes," Emma said.

"We'd also need an adjoining plot," John added, "for Emma's father. He's buried in New York but we've already arranged the paperwork over at the funeral home. I'm told it's not too difficult to arrange."

Emma was startled again. She hadn't gone into the funeral home, and hadn't known he had started on moving her father's remains. This was a man of action. This was a man she could love with all her heart—if he weren't forever picking at her!

"That's no problem," Reverend Hardy continued, in answer to John's remark. "When would you like the service to be held?" She looked questioningly at Emma.

"I don't know," Emma said.

John said, "Normally, a wake at the funeral parlor is held for two days. Then the funeral service follows. Today is Monday, so we would want a funeral service and burial on Wednesday. Will that be all right?"

"Yes," Barbara Hardy said as she nodded her head in assent. "Wednesday morning would be fine. Say around ten o'clock?" She made a cryptic note on her calendar.

"That would be fine. Thank you very much," Emma finally managed to get a word in.

"What time tonight," Reverend Hardy asked, "will the wake be?"

"I'll arrange it with the funeral home," John said. "After the funeral, we'll have a collation at the house."

"I have been ministering in this area for twenty-five years and I can't remember the last time I was in Balleymore," Barbara Hardy said, looking sympathetically at Emma. "My condolences on your loss."

"Thank you for all your help," Emma said as she tried to keep the tears at bay. Good Lord, she was crying like a baby lately!

When they were back in the Jeep, Emma turned to John and said, "Who can I get to prepare all the food and drinks for the collation? I don't think I can ask Mrs. Macrae to do it all."

"I think," John answered, "that if you ask anyone else to do anything but serve Mrs. Macrae will be highly insulted. Just let her work out her grief in her own way. When Mrs. Macrae gets upset she invariably goes to the kitchen and starts to cook. I bet that when we get back to Balleymore she will have treats galore already made for us."

"Are you trying to say that she 'sugarcoats' problems?" Emma asked, trying to get him to smile. That's my mission for the day; perhaps for the rest of my life, she told herself. And then, when he gets the smiling all down pat, I'm going to start kissing him, and when he gets *that* down I'm—I don't know *what* I'm going to do then. From deep down in some hidden recess of her mind a tiny voice said, why don't you marry the man and teach him a sharp lesson?

"That was a terrible pun," John said with a small upturn of his lips. "Wherever did you get that? I certainly hope you keep your day job. You'll never make it as a comedienne."

"Thank you very much," Emma said à la Groucho Marx with his cigar motion. "And now for a word from our local station."

Wednesday was drizzly, rainy, wet. A perfect day for a funeral. The words of the ancient service flowed over her, comforting and heartening. Finally the last words were said and it was time for Emma and Jill to place the first flowers on the coffin as it rested on its webbing above the open grave.

Jill had been crying copiously during the ceremony. She was dressed in a brand-new black dress which fitted her like a glove. The heavy black veil and the black gloves were a trifle ostentatious, Emma thought, but she was not going to judge. Luke led Jill very carefully to the coffin while he held the umbrella over her head. He helped her place the orchid they had brought on the dark wooden lid and then, just as carefully, led her away to his car.

Emma had been more than happy to let Jill go first. She didn't think she was dressed appropriately for a funeral but with all the details to be dealt with she'd had no time to go shopping. So she wore her navy blue suit with a plain, collarless cream blouse. John was holding an enormous black umbrella and it sheltered both of them. She placed the one perfect bloodred rosebud she had found this morning on the lid and then she lingered for a moment to say goodbye to the tormented woman who had been her mother. A shiver ran up her spine. Memories of her father were hazy and very old. The only memories she would have of her mother would be of her deathbed. Now she was truly an orphan. She was grateful when John put an arm around her waist and pulled her close. At least he offered a temporary comfort. Maybe he'd forgive her, some day, for being a Ballentine?

Not many people attended the services. There was another person in the cemetery, a stranger to Emma. She didn't think he had come for the funeral. He was an elderly man, wandering around the Ballentine plot and reading the names of the nearby headstones. He stopped to look at a few and nodded as if greeting them. He paid little attention to the solemn ceremony. Reverend Hardy had kept to the simple service outlined in the Book of Common Prayer and took no notice of him. But Emma wondered.

"Who is that man?" She asked John in an undertone as the mourners began to file out of the burial ground and back to their cars.

"Which man?" John said, also in a hushed tone.

"That little man with the full head of white hair by the headstone with the angel."

When John finally spotted the man in question, the gentleman was heading straight for where they stood. "Thought I'd find you here," the elderly man said to John.

"Mr. Hendricks," John said. "If I had known you wanted to attend the funeral, I'd have offered to come and get you."

"Why should you?" Mr. Hendricks said. "I've got a chauffeur. I came to see what's happening with all of this brouhaha. Now let's go and get out of the rain. I'd like to see Balleymore again. And taste Edna Macrae's sweetbread."

"Emma," John said, "this is Mr. Hendricks. He's the Ballentine family lawyer. Or he *was* the Ballentine family lawyer."

"Hello, my dear," Mr. Hendricks said, all gallant cavalier. "It is a pleasure and honor to meet you. I can see you have the family hair and eyes. My regrets about your mother. She was the most beautiful girl in the county in her day."

"Thank you," Emma said. She tried to retrieve her hand from his warm grasp. "Let's get out of this rain. Do you want to ride with us up to Balleymore?"

"No, thank you," the lawyer said with a gleam. "I'm going to put my overpaid driver to work. Michael, get the car started. We'll follow Mr. Weld up to Balleymore." Michael, a young man of about twenty, hopped to smartly.

"He's related," Emma said, comparing the faces, "isn't he?"

"Yes," the lawyer said, "he's my grandson. He wanted a summer job that paid well and wasn't going to overwork him." He laughed and continued, "I may pay well, but he works for it."

Up at Balleymore, Mrs. Macrae had fixed enough food to feed the county. What we need to do, Emma thought, is not let anyone leave without taking a food packet with them.

The reason for the gathering was depressing enough, but she felt that something was missing. What was it?

"Do you want another drink?" John asked.

"I'm drinking coffee," Emma said. "But thank you, I'd love another cup."

Emma looked at the guests. No one attending showed any grief for the deceased. The missing ingredient was sorrow. The guests who had come to the collation had come out of duty. They were *family retainers*. These were people who worked for the Ballentine estate. People who came out of friendship with John. He knew everybody in the room and they seemed to like him.

Jill and Luke were sitting on the couch in the corner with their heads together. Luke was drinking Scotch and Jill was having a rum and Coke. Mr. Hendricks was talking to Mrs. Macrae over the refreshment table. They seemed to be kindred souls. Dr. Owens and Nurse Snow came by for some coffee and pastries but left early. "Another case," the nurse announced. "There seems to be no end of them." The farmworkers had all come to pay their respects and to meet the two claimants. Who knew? They were waiting for the heir to be named so that they could know their futures. They had some pastries and some coffee. They looked as if they would be leaving *en masse* very soon.

John brought her coffee and stood for a moment by her side. "How are you doing?" he asked.

"I'm all right." Emma sighed. "I didn't know her. She didn't know me. I feel like one of the tenants who came out of respect for the house. What am I supposed to feel like?"

"I don't know. You looked lost in thought. I was a little worried."

"I was thinking that there wasn't anyone at the funeral service here who even cared for her," Emma said, sighing.

"She left these parts for greener pastures. She hurt a great many people in the process. She wasn't a very friendly person. Particularly with those she considered to be beneath her.''

But she did it all for love, Emma thought, remembering those very last few minutes when her mother had seemed to recognize all the havoc she had created. She *thought* she had done it all for love. And then, at the very end, she had almost seemed to realize how wrong she had been. Emma shivered. What about me? she asked herself. Am I liable to repeat my mother's mistakes? She shook the thought off. Her mother had asked for forgiveness. And her daughter had granted it. The past was a closed book. "Why did they come, then," she asked, "if none of them loved her?"

"They came for the sake of the Ballentine name. It means a lot to local people. It always has."

At this point, Jesse Fernandez came up to John. He was John's right-hand man at the Weld farm. He was going to go back to work. He offered his respects to Emma and then asked John if there was anything in particular he wanted done, other than the scheduled activities. "It's a sad day with the rain and all," John told Jesse. "Just finish what's on schedule for today and then go on home. I'll see you all tomorrow."

The small group of tenant farmers who attended milled around aimlessly, as if they couldn't find the door. "What's wrong?" Emma whispered.

"Think," he whispered back. "Just assume that you *are* the new owner of the farm. What would you say to them to reassure them?"

Of course, Emma told herself. "There won't be any changes," she said loudly enough so all could hear. "Things will go on as they have."

The farmworkers smiled in relief, thanked Emma again, and left the house as a group. Across the room

Jill came up out of her chair, furious. "What did you say that for?" she snapped. Emma stepped back from her, fearing more to come. "It was my job to say that!"

"What would you have said?" John said. The weight of his voice crushed the opposition.

Jill and Luke waited until the employees left, and then came over together, holding hands. "I think it's time we cleared up the issue while we have Mr. Hendricks here," Luke said rather forcefully.

"What issue are we talking about?" Mr. Hendricks inquired softly.

"The will, of course," Luke said arrogantly. "And just who inherits this property."

"And what will," the lawyer asked innocently, "are we talking about?"

"The will that Mrs. Ballentine made before her death," Luke stated as if he were addressing a simpleton.

"You'll have to let me see this will. I'll need to probate the document," Mr. Hendricks said. "I'll also need some proof of identification. Your birth certificate, miss. Your father's death certificate. That sort of thing."

"How long will it take to probate?" Luke asked before Jill could protest.

"It depends," Mr. Hendricks said.

"On what?" Luke was insistent.

"Are there any contestants to the will? Are there any legal obligations on the deceased's estate?"

"What do you mean?" Jill asked.

"Are there any debts outstanding, any creditors due, are there any obligations still pending on the estate?" Mr. Hendricks rattled off. "Things of that nature."

"Yes," a voice from the door said loudly and rather unsteadily, "I have a claim on the deceased's estate. She owes me! Where do you keep the booze?" Mr. Weld,

John and Luke's father, stood in the doorway holding on to the casing. "She owed me! I took her out of this dump and showed her a good time. We could've had more, but she ran out of money. Damn woman!"

"Father," John said stonily, "how did you get over here?"

"I drove," Mr. Weld said rather defiantly.

"Oh, my God," John muttered under his breath. He turned to Luke and said, "Could you help me here?"

"Hey," Luke said offhandedly, "you're the elder brother. You took over responsibility. You get to take care of him yourself."

John looked disgustedly at his brother and came to a decision. "Excuse me for a moment. I've got to make a call."

Mr. Weld the elder had managed to maneuver his way over to the drinks cabinet and fix himself a straight Scotch. While he stood there drinking it he had his eyes fixed on Emma. She could feel his eyes boring through her. When John started out of the door, Emma excused herself also and followed along after him.

"I can do this on my own," John said defensively.

"I know you can," she said. "I just wanted to get out of that room. I'm sorry, but your father frightens me."

"Don't be worried. I'll send for someone to come to get him. I wonder how he got out of the house without a set of keys?" The last sentence was said to somewhere in the air. He wasn't talking to her.

They went into the library and he picked up the phone. He dialed a number and waited for someone to answer. It didn't appear that anyone was answering and after a few moments John slammed the receiver down.

"Where are they? It looks as if *I'm* going to have to take him home. Come on, we need to get back to the others."

Why? Emma thought. Why do we have to go back to the others? Two of the people left in there I don't like and two I don't understand. But I surely don't want to be left alone.

"Before we go back," John said with a smile, "I have a small mission to complete."

Before Emma could even ask what he was talking about, he took her in his arms and kissed her. She had been kissed before. Luke had kissed her. But that had been a penny firecracker; this was a rocket booster. She melted into a small puddle at his feet.

"It's nice to know I haven't lost the touch," he muttered when he lifted his lips and let her go. "Come on, before they send out search parties for us."

She followed him down the hall back to the sitting room where the others were gathered, still in a daze. Lost the touch—what did he mean by that?

Nothing had changed in their absence. Mr. Weld was standing in front of the drinks cabinet depleting the supply and still talking about being owed. Luke was still hovering over Jill like a chicken over its prize egg. Mr. Hendricks was still listening to Mrs. Macrae about something. When John and Emma reentered all the movement in the room stopped.

When Emma caught her eye, Mrs. Macrae blushed and smiled and said, "Look at me. I'm just wasting time. I've got to clean up the mess in the kitchen and in here. And get dinner started. Will you be staying, Mr. Hendricks?"

"I can't tonight," Hendricks said with real regret. "I've made other plans for this evening." He turned back to address Jill. "If yours is the only claim on the estate then I can get started right away." Jill beamed at him.

"She isn't the only claimant," John said, cutting into the bubble that surrounded Luke and Jill. "Emma has a claim on the estate too."

"What's in it for you?" Luke snarled at his brother.

"There's nothing in it for me," John snapped back. "Just simple justice."

"Oh, come on," Luke sneered. "Nothing in it for you? While you've been busy making up to Emma? Are you going to make her an offer for the farm? I told her about you and your plans for the valley. How you hate the Ballentines and only want to buy them out of the valley. How are you doing in seducing her? Kissing her in the library? I have to tell you, your plan is working out great! Look at her, she's ready to melt. I'll bet you that you lose. But don't worry. I won't forget the little people who helped me. After we sell this piece of land for the big money the developers are offering, I'll do something for the little people. Even if Emma Elizabeth is the legal heir, she and I we have a deal. I'm going to be her agent in the sale. You lose all the way around!"

Emma came out of her daze and heard the words. "I never said that," she sputtered to Luke. "I never said you could be my agent. I don't want to sell—to anybody! Why are you saying these things?"

Her back stiffened and she glared at Luke—who stood gloating at John, who stood with questions in his eyes for Emma. Everyone else in the room stared at the three of them in shock. Jill was stunned. She stared at her fiancé with large bewildered eyes.

John was the first to break the tableau. He moved over to the drinks cabinet, took his father by the arm and walked him out of the door. The old man was still mumbling about debts and family secrets. Their departure was a signal for Mr. Hendricks to start off on his own.

"But you can't go yet," Jill wailed as if she'd just come back to earth. "What about the will?"

"I presume you have a will," the lawyer said. "If I may have all those papers and anything related, I'll see if I can study them over the next few days, and arrange a meeting to discuss the situation."

"Several days?" Jill looked at him with her eyes wide-open. "Several days? We can't wait that long. Mrs. Ballentine wouldn't want us to wait that long."

"You don't understand," Mr. Hendricks said. "This looks like a long and complicated matter. And Mrs. Ballentine has all the time in the world to settle her problems—now."

"What do I do for money in the meantime?" Jill asked anxiously.

The lawyer shrugged his shoulders. "I'm sure the conservator of the estate can make some advance payments to keep you afloat. Of course, should you prove not to be the heir you'll have to return all that—and anything else the estate may have advanced to you."

"Oh, my God," Luke muttered.

"Oh, my God," Emma muttered under her breath. The mad urge to flee settled into her brain, but before she could get to the door she heard the roar of the Jeep's motor. It was too late to ask John any questions. Why had he kissed her in the library? Did he not hate her any more for whatever reason? She needed desperately to find something to believe in, and she'd prefer it to be John.

Luke and Jill were squabbling in low voices in front of her. Emma sidled around them and went to join Mrs. Macrae.

"Hendricks has thrown the cat among the pigeons," that worthy said as she took Emma's hand in her own.

"Good afternoon, all," Mr. Hendricks called above the rising storm.

"And look how much he's enjoying it," Mrs. Macrae said. "Come to the kitchen, lass, and let's have a cup of tea."

CHAPTER SEVEN

ALL THE way back to the Weld property John asked himself where he had gone wrong. He had kissed her because it had seemed like the right thing to do and that kiss in the library had been world-class. She had responded like a wild tigress. He had forgotten his hatred of the Ballentines and had only been aware of Emma. Something had gone wrong after that. She didn't honestly believe Luke, did she? The last thing on his mind where Emma was concerned was Balleymore. He had enough to do with his own farm. He looked forward with keen anticipation to turning Balleymore over to Emma. That was as long as she didn't sell to the developers. He was more than willing to be responsible for Emma Ballentine and he didn't really care if she owned the property or not.

Emma Ballentine? Let me count the ways: tall and beautiful. Intelligent. Tender and compassionate. Makes me feel good just to be near her. Fits into my arms perfectly. Soft skin. Magnificent figure.

Luckily for him, there was no traffic on the narrow road to his family house. His attention had been on Emma all the way, and not on the road. His father was unconscious during the drive. Steaming drunk, for which John was thankful. He had a strong sense of duty; his father rated poorly on the "duty" scale.

His father would have wound up on the street had not John rushed to the rescue. The old man had mortgaged the family land, which he did not own, and then tried to party his way through the mortgage money. Luckily for him John had stepped in at that point. Not for his father's sake, but for the family name and farm.

John was a farmer at heart. He enjoyed the work. He loved watching the crops grow. With money he had inherited from his maternal grandfather he had bought back the mortgages and set the Weld farm in order. Hard work had earned a profit, and now the farm was a moneymaker.

His father felt that the world owed him a living. A rich living. So John tried to keep him at the farm, and out of his way. And sometimes it worked. But how in God's world can I reconcile my father and Emma? he wondered now. And if she can't stand my father, can she stand me?

He stopped the Jeep at the front door. Luckily, Jesse Fernandez, his assistant manager, was waiting for him. "Help me get him up to bed, Jesse?" And then out to the gardens, to try to subdue his problems by hard work.

At seven o'clock that evening John was exhausted. He felt every one of his thirty-six years, and a few that might belong to someone else. It had been a *long* day. It was time to sit down and relax.

He took his beer and went to sit on the veranda off the back of the house. He had not seen Luke since the wake but he wasn't going to worry about his brother any further. He had other plans to make. He picked up the portable phone he had brought outside with him and dialed the Balleymore number.

"Hello, Ballentine residence," Mrs. Macrae answered.

"Hello, Mrs. Macrae," John replied. "May I speak to Emma?"

"Just hold on a moment," Mrs. Macrae said. "I think she's in the library. I'll go and get her."

"Thank you," John said.

"Yes?" Emma's voice came over the line. "What do you want?" He could hear the challenge in her tone.

"I was thinking of going over to Deerfield tomorrow. Would you care to come with me?"

"Why should I want to go anywhere with you?" Emma asked suspiciously. "Is this part of your operation to get in with the heiress to Balleymore? What if I'm not the heiress? Wouldn't this all be a waste of time?"

"Emma," John grumbled, "don't believe everything my brother tells you. I'm going into town for supplies. I thought you might like to see Deerfield. Get out of the house for a while."

"Oh," said Emma, sounding just a little ashamed of herself. "I'm sorry for being so short. My nerves are pretty much shot with all that's happened lately. Yes, I'd like to get out of the house. What time do you want to leave?"

They arranged a time and said goodbye. John would have liked to continue talking to her but he had heard the stress in her voice. How was he going to get her to trust him? Slow and easy, the old Spanish cliché. *Poco a poco.* This was just the first step.

Back at Balleymore, Emma sat by the phone in the hallway. She was confused. There was too much about John Weld that baffled her. There were moments when she was convinced that he was only after Balleymore. That was, if she was the "correct" Emma Ballentine. He went from hating her to kissing her. There were moments when she was more than willing to melt into his kisses. What was it about this man that confused her so badly?

"What's the matter?" Jill asked as she went by Emma in the hallway. Jill sounded as if she really cared, but Emma wasn't about to share her troubles. Her years as a foster child had taught her to keep her feelings to herself.

"Nothing," Emma said. "I was just thinking about my next book's plot."

"What do you write?"

"Murder mysteries," Emma said. "I think I'll kill five or ten people here at Balleymore." Jill didn't look *that* interested.

"Do you sell a lot of books?" asked Jill

"I have, according to my editor, a great deal of reader appeal. And it's been helped by having three of my earlier books on the bestseller list."

"Oh," Jill said when it was obvious that Emma had finished. "I want to be rich enough that I could waste money if I wanted to. I'm tired of being poor. I want to be rich. I was just asking if you made money at writing," she continued, "because I like you. I've been poor and it's no fun."

"That's very kind of you," Emma said with a straight face. "What are you going to do if you inherit the estate?"

"I'm gonna sell it to the developers for all the money I can get," Jill explained, "and then I'm packing up and going to the Riviera. That's in France, you know. Yeah. Luke and me will be on the Riviera. After I get my inheritance, Luke and me, we're gonna get married. Only I'm making sure that the money is all mine. If Luke wants any, he'll have to ask me for it. That way, he won't run around."

"You've certainly thought this all out, haven't you?" Emma said gently.

"I know what I want," Jill said. "I want the money and I want Luke Weld. I'm gonna get both of them. So don't stand in my way and don't fall for any of Luke's talk."

"I beg your pardon?" Emma said stiffly. She was astonished that Jill had known about Luke's advances and had never said anything.

"Oh, c'mon," Jill said forcefully. "Don't think that I don't know Luke's trying to play both sides of the fence. He wants to cover his bets. Just don't fall for any of his lines. He's a rotten man but he's mine!"

"Please," Emma said, "believe me when I say he's *all* yours."

"Just as long as you understand," Jill said as she started down the corridor. "I'd just hate to have to hurt you, but I would."

Oh, I understand, Emma said to herself. Hands off. Well, my dear, he's all yours! Don't worry about me poaching. What I don't understand is why you're staying with him. Particularly when you don't trust him any more than I do. Oh, well, if nothing else, I may use you in a book.

She stood up and went up the stairs to her room. "I'll sleep well tonight," she told herself. But she didn't.

When Emma got up the next morning she knew that the day would live up to the forecast. It was going to be sunny and hot. After her shower, she dressed in a short-sleeved cotton camp shirt that matched her khaki walking shorts, slipped on her matching espadrilles and skipped down the stairs. It was hard not to be happy. She looked forward to being with John. She might not trust him any more than Jill trusted Luke, but he was exciting to be around. Maybe there's not so much difference between Jill and me? Sisters under the skin? she thought.

"Good morning, Mattie," she sang as she entered the kitchen. "What's for breakfast? Can I help?"

"I don't know what's to help, dearie," Mrs. Macrae said with a smile. "There's only you and me to cook for this morning. Miss Jill went out late last night with Mr. Luke. I guess they went out looking for a good time—and found it."

"What's the matter?" Emma asked. She was concerned not so much with what Mattie was saying but the way she was saying it. Mrs. Macrae had been her ally since she came to Balleymore. She was Emma's only true friend in the area, and Emma knew the value of a good friend.

"Nothing," Mrs. Macrae said. "It's nothing for you to worry about." With forced cheerfulness she continued, "I thought we'd have Belgian waffles with strawberries. What do you say to that?"

"Is there any other way to have Belgian waffles?" Emma said. "I'd love it. I'll set the table."

As she worked Emma looked over at Mattie and she found herself being watched. She motioned with the coffeepot toward Mattie's cup and Mattie shook her head.

"Not right now, dearie," the older woman said. "So, what are your plans for today?"

"I'm supposed to be going into Deerfield with John this morning. He's going in for supplies and invited me to go and see the town. I've been reading a book about Deerfield and the Indian raids during the King Philip War. I'm looking forward to seeing it."

"I'm glad you and Mr. John are getting on better."

"I'm not sure we are." Emma filled her own coffee mug. "This may just be a truce. Any way it goes, I'd like to see Deerfield."

"I think," Mattie said, "that you should go out and have a wonderful day. Enjoy yourself with Mr. John. He's such a nice boy."

"Mattie," Emma said with deep affection, "I might not be the correct Emma, but even if I'm not I want you to know that you'll always have a place with me. Even if it's not with John."

"That's lovely, Emma," Mattie said. There were tears in her eyes. "But you *are* my little Emma. All you have to do is convince everybody else that you are. That way you inherit all of the Ballentine land. It'd be a real crime if there weren't any Ballentines at Balleymore." And at just that moment John walked into the kitchen. Emma felt her heart skip a beat. He looked so—virile, so altogether masculine. If only he would say something like, Come on, Emma, let's get married.

Instead he looked down at the table with the remains of breakfast and said, "Got any more of those Belgian waffles? I'm starving."

"Don't they feed you at your house?" Emma asked, hiding her disappointment. Mattie bustled off to fix his waffles.

"I ate breakfast this morning," John said as he got himself a cup of coffee. "But that was several hours ago and I've been working hard since then. Even if I hadn't, Mrs. Macrae's waffles are one of the culinary wonders of the county."

Mrs. Macrae handed him a plate with an enormous waffle and mumbled something about not talking that kind of foolishness. The waffle plate was a piece of art, the waffle golden brown, the strawberries a cheery red and the whipped cream a pure snow white. If Emma weren't so full from her own breakfast, she would have asked for another.

"Thank you." John smiled up at Mrs. Macrae and grabbed his fork. "Just remember, if you get tired of being here, I can use you at my place."

For that smile, Emma thought, any woman would roll over and beg. What was it about this man that defied definition? He wasn't, strictly speaking, the best-looking man she had ever seen. But whatever he had, Emma was attracted to it. Violently attracted. And that was something no sensible woman would ever let him know!

"Well, why don't we hit the road? Do you have everything you need?"

"I need to get my hat and sunscreen," Emma said as she jumped up from the table. Anything to get away from his studied gaze.

"Mr. John," Mrs. Macrae said as they watched Emma run, "that girl *is* my Emma. I don't want you to forget what I said. Be kind to her. She hasn't had much kindness in her life. She's a good girl and she deserves to be happy. There has got to be a way to prove that she's the Ballentine girl to the lawyers and everybody."

"Mrs. Macrae," John said with genuine feeling, "*I think* she is Emma. You think she is Emma. I just hope that all of her bits and pieces of paper will prove us correct. And I'll keep your threat in mind."

Emma was coming down the staircase when the front door opened. Luke and Jill came staggering inside.

"We had a perfectly marvelous time," Jill said. "We met people. The *right* people. They're gonna come stay with us when we go to the Riviera. Isn't that so, honey?" She swayed toward Luke, who laughed and nodded agreement.

"Are you as drunk as she is?" John asked his brother.

"Nobody," Luke said, "could be as drunk as she is. She doesn't handle her liquor well. What's the hassle? We're both adults. We can take care of ourselves. Don't play at being my big brother."

"I think I'm gonna be sick," Jill whispered urgently. Her face had suddenly turned an odd shade of green.

Mrs. Macrae sprang into action and took her by the arm to the downstairs bathroom.

"That girl," Luke said, with a smirk, "shouldn't ought to drink so much."

"If she shouldn't, why are you taking her places where she does?" Emma said angrily.

"Why not?" Luke said. "She's my fiancée. No one's forcing her." He leered over at Emma. "You should come and play with me some day soon. That is, if Johnny boy there hasn't already moved in. He wants this property. He knows that I've got Jill wrapped up. So the only other way to get Balleymore is if you turn out to be the heiress. I imagine that's why he's hanging close to you."

Suddenly, Emma felt dirty. The look on Luke's face didn't match the expensive Armani suit and silk shirt he was wearing. She had seen that look before. It made her skin crawl. She backed away from Luke and into John's arms.

"Just go and sit down, brother," John said with disgust. "I've got to figure out how to get you home."

"I can drive," Luke said defensively. "I got us here, didn't I? Oh, by the way, I'm gonna need some cash to repair the front fender and headlight."

"Then you'll damn well have to earn it," John said bluntly. "Your free ride is over, *brother*." An astonished look flashed across Luke's face.

"I'm sorry about this," John said to Emma. "But I've got to get him home. I can't allow him to drive in his condition. Maybe we should just call this trip off."

"I'd still like to go to Deerfield," Emma said, thinking quickly. "Why does he have to go to your place? Why can't he sleep it off here? We have extra rooms. We even have one with a lock."

"I don't want to saddle anyone with him," John stated.

"Please," Emma pleaded. "This won't be an imposition. I'd really like to get out of the house."

"Well—okay."

They all turned to look at Luke. He was sitting down on the bottom step of the staircase, half asleep. It looked like an impossible job to move him, but John took Luke's arm across his shoulder and walked him up the stairs as if he were a featherweight. Emma followed behind to help. They finally got Luke into Mrs. Ballentine's room and onto the bed. As they left the room, Luke was mumbling something. Emma wasn't at all sure she wanted to know what he was saying. They closed the door behind them just as Mrs. Macrae came around the corner and met them.

"I've just poured the other one into her bed. You have yours in there? They should be out for the count. Now, you two be on your way. You deserve a day out, Emma. Go on. I can handle these two."

"Are you sure?" Emma asked.

"Yes. Now *git!*"

John grabbed Emma's hand and towed her down the staircase. Emma picked up her bag from the sideboard in the front hallway as she was pulled along. They came out of the house and walked through the dappled sunlight to the Jeep. Just before she got into it Emma took a deep breath and smiled a big smile.

"Are you happy?" John asked.

"It's a beautiful day," Emma said. "The sun is smiling. I feel at home. Yes, I'm happy."

"Well," John said after a short silence. "Good. Now let's get this show on the road before some other disaster occurs."

The trip to Deerfield was quickly done. Emma spent the time watching the countryside. She had driven to Balleymore on the highway, so all this back-road travel was new to her. It was easy to see why both the Native Americans and the white settlers would have fought over this land. In her reading, she had come across the Ballentine family name rather often. If this was her family, she thought, I'm proud to be a member. Even if I'm not, I'm going to claim membership anyway, she told herself, chuckling. Maybe she could write a book about it? Now that was an idea.

They rolled into Deerfield around eleven o'clock. John pulled the Jeep over to the side and turned to face Emma. "Do you want to eat lunch first, or can we go and get my errands done?"

"After that big breakfast?" Emma laughed. "I'm not hungry, so let's go get your supplies."

"A rose in the desert," John murmured as he turned and drove down the street to the right.

"Hmm?" Emma asked. "What did you say?"

"Nothing. I was just talking to myself."

They reached the warehouse and accomplished their errand in record time, according to John.

"Look, it only took us about an hour and a half."

"If you say so," Emma said sceptically. "It seemed awfully slow to me. But I guess for people who wait for leaves to sprout it was quick."

"Was that a slur on us farming people?" John asked with mock affront. "I may have to report you to the union. Just be careful. Are you ready for lunch yet?"

"Yes," Emma said. "Now that you mention it, I am getting hungry. But—I didn't bring any money with me."

"I was going to pay for the meal," John said. "After all, I invited you to lunch."

"That is not part of the chauffeur's duties," Emma said with determination in her voice.

"I'm not just the chauffeur," John said. "I had planned all along to feed you. We have a branch of the Monty's restaurant chain here. Don't think of this as a meal but as repayment for all the times I've eaten at Balleymore."

"This wouldn't be the first step in a seduction campaign, would it? Feed the girl up and then——" She was joking, but when she looked over at John she was amazed to see how serious he was.

"That's why I have trouble getting along with women," he grumbled. "The idea never crossed my mind!" Emma stared at him. Was there the tiniest bit of a smile lurking around those lips? Did he actually have a sense of humor?

"The Monty's restaurant chain was founded here in Deerfield," John said. "We'll be dining at the original."

"That sounds fine," Emma said. "I'll have to think about your treating me, but I'll be glad to go and eat."

Without another word, John started the engine and drove out of the warehouse parking lot. The Jeep now had a strong aroma of dirt and plant supplement. Emma made sure her window was open. John drove about four blocks and there it was, an old metal dining car with a large addition in the back. There was a large neon sign on the roof of the metal diner that read, "MONTY'S DINER. THE WORLD'S BEST HAMBURGERS.

"Are we going to sit here in awe," John said, "or shall we eat?"

"Lead on, Macduff."

"Him again? There aren't many Scots families in the area. Mostly old Yankee, Italian, and Portuguese." And this time, as she stole a look, there definitely *was* a little upturn to the corner of his mouth.

Emma sat there looking at him with a gentle smile on her face. He wondered if her lips tasted as good as he remembered. He leaned toward her and she toward him, and their lips met in the middle. It was a soft kiss, full of promise and hope.

When they pulled apart, the softness went out of Emma's eyes. She was recalling the times John had changed on her. You may be in love with him, but he wants Balleymore, she told herself. "Let's go eat lunch," she said in a strained voice.

"All right," John said. His mind spun. Yet another time she's turned from hot to cold. What's gone wrong this time?

They climbed the stairs into the restaurant, side by side but not holding hands. "Look, there's Dr. Owens," John said. "Do you mind if I ask him to eat with us?"

"No," Emma said, "not at all." She was more than happy to have somebody else at the table with them. She was too nervous to be alone with John.

"Doc," John greeted the rumpled, elderly man in the brown suit. "Fancy meeting you here. Are you with someone or would you like to eat with Emma and me?"

"I'd be glad of the company." Dr. Owens smiled up at John. His gaze shifted to Emma, and smiled at her too. Dr. Owens was blessed with his smile. It took this rather ordinary little man who dressed badly and made him a man to trust with your life. It was the smile a politician would give his eyeteeth for.

"Started to clean out my records today," he announced. "All the pediatric records. I've got all the records I have on Emma Ballentine ready for you, John. That's what you asked for, isn't it?"

"Yes," John said. "We need anything you can provide. Such as?"

"If you're Emma," Dr. Owens said to her, "did you outgrow your allergies or do you have to take shots?"

"Well," Emma replied, "I *am* Emma Ballentine, and I still have allergies. I don't take shots any more, but I have a bottle of pills that would choke a horse. Mainly, I try to avoid things that give me a reaction."

The place was crowded but the hostess found them a booth at the back. The restaurant smelled of broiling burgers and the blue plate special, lobster rolls. The management had set up a broiler grill that faced the customers and kept up the illusion of being in an old-fashioned diner. The waitress was there almost immediately with their silverware and glasses of water.

"Your menus are in the rack," the waitress said and pointed at the end of the table. There was a small jukebox attached to the wall at the end of the table over the menus and condiments. "Take your time. Or are you ready to order now?"

"Do you want a burger?" John asked both the doctor and Emma. They both nodded vigorously. John ordered the hamburger platter for each of them with iced tea to drink. The waitress hurried off to the grill with the order, leaving the luncheon trio in the booth.

Emma sat with an entranced look on her face as she inspected the interior décor. The floor and tabletops were turquoise and the booth benches and chairs were upholstered in magenta pink. The waitresses were in uniforms that matched those colors. At the counter in front of the grill the milkshake machines were busily chugging away. The two countermen were moving as if they had choreographed their movements. In fact, everything about the service was moving with both skill and assurance. The waitress was back quickly with their tea.

John put a spoonful of sugar into his drink. "Well, what do you think?" he asked Emma. "Is it as good as the one back in New York?"

"Staten Island," Emma replied. "Every Monty's is good and I recommend them to anyone who asks. Do you have a quarter? I see a song on the jukebox I haven't heard in a long time."

"Here you go." John handed over one or two coins. He watched as she inserted the coin and very carefully punched in her selection. "You get three selections for your money. You'll have to choose two more."

"Do you have a favorite?" Emma asked him.

"I like B6," he said with a smile.

"All right. And you, Doctor, do you have a favorite song?"

"Unless they have 'Red Sails in the Sunset,'" Dr. Owens said, "I have no favorites."

"That's F12," John said before Emma could look up the song title.

"I get the feeling that you come here frequently," Emma said with a smile. "At least, often enough to have memorized the song list."

"I have a very good memory," John said solemnly. "Besides, they haven't changed the music in the past year or so."

Emma punched in the other two selections just as the waitress appeared back at the table with the three hamburger platters.

"Do you need anything else?" the waitress asked with a smile. At the murmured "no, thanks" she nodded and moved away to clean a table.

The hamburger platter consisted of an enormous hamburger patty on a kaiser roll with lettuce and tomato slices. The rest of the plate was filled with fresh French fries. Emma had always felt that a meal at Monty's could feed a small army. It was definitely too much for an ordinary person to eat by herself. And so much for my gourmet eating, she told herself as she added ketchup to her burger and chuckled as both John and the doctor did the same thing. John then reached for the vinegar and sprinkled some on his fries.

"I've never seen anyone put vinegar on French fries before," she said.

"That's because you grew up in New York," he said as he popped a fry in his mouth. "People in New York have no idea about good food. You even ruin clam chowder. Who ever heard of clam chowder with tomatoes?"

"You people in New England think that you invented taste and seafood. It just took us New Yorkers to correct your mistakes."

The doctor very carefully stayed out of the discussion but Emma and John both enjoyed the friendly arguing as to the superiority of their own region's cooking. They were about halfway through their meals when the doctor's buzzer sounded. He sighed regretfully as he looked at the number displayed on the readout screen. "Sorry, folks, but it looks as if I'm needed."

"I'm sorry you didn't get to finish your meal," Emma commented.

"Don't worry," he said, "I'm going to take it with me. I've eaten more than either of you two." He gave them both a reflective look. "Got to get married one of these days," he added. "Of course, I wasn't defending anybody's cooking. See you both later." He picked up the remainder of his burger and carried it out of the door with him. Emma noticed that he didn't stop at the cash register. Perhaps it was because he was a doctor?

"I like him," Emma said.

"Just about everybody likes him," John said. "He's a local landmark. He's been doctoring here for most of his life. His folks come from Deerfield and he came back to practice here after the Great War."

"In 1917? He's getting on, isn't he?"

"He's not *that* old," John answered. "I'm talking about 1945. But he has brought in a young doctor to pass the business over to. Unfortunately for Dr. Weston, not many of the old-timers are ready to rely on him while Dr. Owens is still around."

"And he has my childhood medical records," Emma mused.

When they had finished and were ready to leave, John picked up the bill the waitress had dropped on their table.

"How much do I owe you?" she asked John as they got up from the booth.

"Nothing," John said as he left a hefty tip on the table. "This was my treat. You can pay next time." He left Emma behind as he walked out of the door. She tried to work up a little indignation, but it was impossible. Still murmuring to herself, she followed him out to the Jeep.

"I could have paid for my meal," she told him as she sat back in the seat.

He looked down at her as he turned on the ignition. "I don't know any woman in the valley who could outpay you." They returned to Balleymore in a silence which wasn't broken until he stopped the Jeep at the front door. And all during the trip her mind worked on a little tape. Now what did he mean by that? But she had no answer.

"I want to thank you for the beautiful day," she said softly as she squirmed out of the door.

"You're welcome. Mrs. Macrae said you deserved a happy day. I hope you had one."

"Oh, I did," Emma said, startled. "Do you still hate me because I'm a Ballentine?"

"Where in the world did you get that idea?" John asked. "As long as you don't act like your mother——"

"Thanks a lot," Emma said through clenched teeth. "I'm getting very tired of being accused of being my mother's daughter. If I'm just like my mother, why aren't you just like your father? I keep asking myself how I could have fallen in love with such a small-minded person!"

CHAPTER EIGHT

EMMA turned on her heel and marched into the house, slamming the big front door behind her. Sometimes, she wanted him so badly—just to get even. What a monster! She had read somewhere of someone who was described as setting grudges in cement. Maybe they were talking about John Weld.

She continued to stand in the front hall getting angrier and angrier. Mrs. Macrae came out of the kitchen carrying a tall glass of lemonade. The old lady flinched at the look on Emma's face.

"Here," the housekeeper said, handing her the glass, "you look as if you need this. Is something wrong?"

"Nothing," Emma said. "Nothing. I'm so darned exasperated. Why am I so attracted to a man who wants to pigeonhole me? He wants me to be like my mother so that he can hate me with impunity. Mattie, I love him. Why doesn't he like me?" The last sentence was said with a wail as she burst into tears.

Mrs. Macrae wore a confused and worried look on her face. "Oh, my dear. I don't know what to say that could help you. Mr. John is usually a very even-tempered person. I thought he was over his hatred for the Ballentines." She paused and nibbled on her lip before continuing. "What did he do to you?"

"He kissed me! Twice! And then he said that I de served a happy day as long as I didn't act like my mother!" Emma said indignantly. "I told him that I

140

wouldn't act like my mother as long as he didn't act like his father."

"Now there, Emma," Mrs. Macrae said, sounding shocked, "Mr. John is the most honest man I know. Unfortunately, he sometimes says things he doesn't really mean. I'm sure there must be an explanation."

"If there is," Emma said glumly, "I'd sure like to hear it."

"I don't know what's eating you," Mrs. Macrae said soothingly, "but I'm sure there's an excellent reason for everything Mr. John does."

Emma heard the stress in Mattie's voice and decided to drop the subject for the moment. "All right. If you say so." Emma smiled at the older woman. "How's your day been going?"

"I've not heard a peep from either of the two upstairs," Mrs. Macrae said. "But then again, I've been cleaning the pantry shelves and I make a lot of noise doing that."

"Do you need some help?" Emma offered.

"No, thank you." Mrs. Macrae smiled at her. "I've done all I'm going to for today. Oh, you got a registered letter today. Now, where did I put it?" She patted her pockets both in her dress and her apron. "I know I signed for it. Now, where did I put it?"

Emma, acting on instinct, looked on the table in the front hall. There were two registered letters resting on its top. One was addressed to "Ms. Emma Jill Ballentine" and the other to "Ms. Emma Elizabeth Ballentine."

"Here they are, Mattie." She picked up the letter addressed to herself. As she looked at the front of the envelope, she noticed that it was from Mr. Hendricks' office. "It's from Mr. Hendricks," she called. "I wonder what he wants now?"

"Open it," Mrs. Macrae said, "and find out. Put the both of us out of our misery."

"All right." Emma ripped open the top of the envelope and withdrew a sheet of formal paper. It was a summons to appear in the county probate court in six days' time. Mr. Hendricks had petitioned the court to hear on the inheritance. The court of the Commonwealth of Massachusetts was going to meet on Thursday to decide the matter. This piece of information sent a chill down Emma's spine. I'm not sure, she thought, that I want to know who inherits. If they decide too soon I won't have a reason to see John any longer. Even if he's so back and forth about how he thinks of me, I'm committed to him—darn fool that I am!

I need the world to stop for a couple of days so I can adjust to all of the changes in my life, she thought. I'm just beginning to feel as if I belong at Balleymore. It's an odd feeling. I've lived most of my life as a ward of some court. And now here I belong, as I've never belonged before. I like belonging. I don't want that changed. Not so soon!

"I've heard and read about the great delays and backlog of cases in the American judicial system. Why did it have to become efficient all of a sudden? I know that life isn't. It's just that in my case the deck must be stacked. I don't want victory. All I want is a little delay. Just a little delay."

"Don't worry," Mattie said. "The lord will provide."

Oh, well, Emma told herself, get used to it. I can't change anything by crying. I must be one of the most unlucky people in the world. I've been unlucky since I was five and Daddy left me. I've had a lot of experience with heartbreak. I may not like it, but I've got a lot of experience with it.

She used a finger to still a tear. But never with so great a heartache as this. She sighed.

As if from a great distance she could hear Mrs. Macrae saying her name. "Emma?" Mattie was saying. "Is something wrong? What does it say?"

"It's a summons to appear in probate court for a hearing regarding the inheritance of the estate. Mr. Hendricks scheduled a court date. We have to appear next Wednesday."

"I'm coming with you," Mrs. Macrae stated firmly as if she was afraid Emma would tell her no.

"Yes," Emma said distractedly. "Of course. You should come." She paused for a moment and then, as if she had come back down to earth, added, "Please come, if just to hold my hand." She smiled at Mattie with true affection and trust. She was thankful for at least one person she could count on.

Mattie took her hand and stretched up to kiss her cheek. "I missed your growing up, Emma," Mattie said. "I'll be darned if I'll miss the rest of your life."

"Oh, my dear," Emma said with laughter in her voice. "You're my dragon slayer! Now that's cleared up, what's for dinner? I'm starving!"

"What would you like?" Mrs. Macrae asked with a big bright smile. There was almost nothing she liked better than feeding people. With Emma, she not only got to cook for someone who appreciated her cooking, but for someone she loved. "I've nothing defrosted. I thought Mr. John would feed you up."

"He tried," Emma admitted. "But, for some reason or another, I'm hungry again."

"Come into my parlor," Mrs. Macrae said in a deep voice. "We'll see what's available."

Six days later, Emma stood with Mrs. Macrae in the lobby of the probate court building. Like most courthouses, it was made of granite, with cold marble floors. Emma was dressed in a new outfit, an olive short suit with a jacket and matching walking shorts. Just what the fashion merchants were pushing this season. Emma had never bought anything like it before, but she had gone shopping with Jill two days previously. Jill had seen the suit and persuaded Emma to buy it. The jersey top worn under the jacket was beginning to stick to her back, while her feet in the new sandals she had bought the same day were cold.

This must be how Alice felt after going through the Looking Glass, Emma told herself. I'm expecting the White Rabbit to appear, looking at his watch and muttering, "I'm late. I'm late." She was feeling whimsical this morning. Her somewhat odd sense of humor was definitely not helping.

She hadn't slept well the night before. She kept having dreams. All right, she said to herself, admit it! You were dreaming of John. White picket fences, children that looked like their father—and they all looked like John. At the same time, she wanted to know who the court would say was the heir to Balleymore. No matter which way the judgment goes, she thought, I lose. If I'm not the heir, I go back to new York and get on with my life. If I am the heir, I lose John because he'll want me only for the inheritance and hate me because of my parents. Either way it goes, I lose. Damn, damn, damn. She very rarely swore, but she knew the words and felt entitled at this moment.

"Earth calling Emma," John's voice came to her consciousness. "Come in, Emma."

"What?" she said, startled. "Did you say something? I'm sorry, I *was* in outer space. Are you mission control?"

"Yes," John said. "Mr. Hendricks is motioning us to go over to him at that door."

They moved across the marble floor with Mrs. Macrae in tow. When they reached the lawyer he smiled at all of them and asked, "Where's the other claimant? I thought I told you both to be here by now."

"I'm sure she'll be along soon," Emma said. "They won't start without her, will they?"

"Yes, they will," Mr. Hendricks said. "As soon as the case that's in front of the judge now is settled or adjourned, we're on. Judge Harper doesn't like to be kept waiting. I don't like to be kept waiting. When you get to be my age, you can't waste it waiting for people." He sounded almost peevish. He shook his head and called over to his grandson and chauffeur, "Michael, go outside and see if Jill Ballentine is out there. If she is, tell her to march herself right in here. Now." At his grandfather's barked order, "young" Michael started toward the large glass doors.

He got to the doors just in time to open them for Jill and Luke. When they saw the small crowd with the lawyer they hurried over. Jill was in a pale pink sundress that at the same time was demure, feminine and revealing. Emma couldn't understand how any dress could do that. Perhaps it was just Jill's petite figure. All Emma could do was look in envy. Anyway, they were here. Emma could have done without Luke's presence, but he'd brought Jill.

"All right," Mr. Hendricks said. "Now that we're all here... I am the lawyer for the estate. I don't represent either of the two claimants. What I'm going to do is present my findings to the judge and she'll make the decision." He looked at both Emma and Jill in turn and he saw a question on Jill's face. "No. I don't know who will be recognized as the heir. I don't care, actually. All I want to do is get rid of this business so I can retire. This is it. My last case. My last responsibility." He sounded cheerful.

Suddenly, the door to the courtroom opened and people started to leave the room. One was saying, angrily, to another who smirked, "I'll appeal! You can't get away with this. What did you do to my grandfather? He was ninety-five if he was a day! He should have left that painting to the immediate family, not some second cousin."

Emma was startled by this remark, said loud enough to have been heard in Balleymore, twenty-seven miles away. "There ain't nothing worse than family when it comes to inheriting," Mr. Hendricks said in an undertone. "Those are the people most willing to stick a knife in your back. Families fight over the darndest things.

"Let's go in, people," he continued as the bailiff motioned them in. "Let's get this show on the road."

Inside the courtroom the bailiff announced the case and judge, and she and Mr. Hendricks started talking in legalese. Emma was slowly falling asleep. Then she heard her name, "Emma Ballentine." Her head snapped up and she started to listen with some interest. Both she and Jill rose at the judge's request to give, under oath, their full and legal names.

"Emma Elizabeth Ballentine."

"Emma Jill Ballentine."

"Your Honor," Mr. Hendricks addressed the court. "We have in this case two individuals claiming to be the daughter of Edward Everett Ballentine, late of Balleymore Farm in this county, and his wife Emma Julia Ballentine, also deceased. Therefore, each claims to be the direct heir and beneficiary of the estate in question. Both of the claimants have introduced death certificates for Edward Everett Ballentine. Initial inspection indicates that each of the documents could be true, but not both. After investigation, we have found that the death certificate of Edward Everett Ballentine who is alleged to have died in New York City earlier this year is registered in the New York City Hall of Records. The other death certificate is unregistered in the county of alleged origin."

He paused to catch his breath, and laid the documents on the judge's low desk. "In addition, I have brought with me a certified copy of the divorce agreement made between Edward Everett and Emma Julia Ballentine." He passed another set of documents up to the judge. "As you can see, Emma Julia was awarded five hundred thousand dollars as settlement in claim for divorce instead of property. She thereafter renounced any claim to the property known as Balleymore."

The judge glanced through the papers, and then looked down at Emma and Jill in turn. "Go on."

"I would like now to call John Weld to the stand. Mr. Weld is acting as the conservator of the estate at the request of the court. I would like him to give the court a report on the financial standing of the Ballentine estate."

John's name was called and he went forward. He was sworn in and stood facing the bench.

"Please give your name and standing in this case."

"My name is John Nichols Weld. I own and live at Weld Farm of this county. I was appointed by the court to be the conservator of the Ballentine estate while the court was searching for an heir at law."

"Are you prepared to give the court an accounting of your administration of this estate at this time?"

"Yes, Your Honor," John said. He smiled at the judge and went on, "The estate was heavily mortgaged when I took over as conservator. It has been paying off these mortgages for nineteen years. Next year will be the last year of the mortgage at which time it will be paid in full. The remainder of monies for the estate go to taxes, normal upkeep and maintenance. The principle value of the estate lies in the acreage known as Balleymore, composed of two hundred and seventy acres, which are valued by the assessors' office at one hundred and fifty thousand dollars. Adding the value of the house and the farm equipment, the total comes to two million, one hundred thousand dollars. I brought a copy of last quarter's tax payment request and a copy of last quarter's tax payment."

The judge frowned down at the financial statements as Hendricks added them to the pile.

Mr. Hendricks paused for a moment, and then moved to a new subject. "Your Honor, I am submitting the holograph will of Emma Julia Ballentine which names Emma Jill Ballentine as her legal heir. It is the duty of the court to decide if Emma Julia Ballentine died with any estate to leave to the so named beneficiary. It is also the duty of the court to decide if, in fact, the so named Emma Jill Ballentine is the sole daughter and therefore, legal heir and beneficiary of Edward Everett Ballentine."

Another pause, as the old lawyer reached into another pocket of his jacket, like a magician pulling rabbits out.

"In addition, I have a holographic will alleged to have been written by the said Edward Everett Ballentine. It is not witnessed and very short. In an effort to prove the validity of this last will I have hired the services of handwriting experts to compare this document with others known to have been written by Edward Everett Ballentine. These experts have been subpoenaed and will be available to the court tomorrow, but the gist of their report is included in the certified report." Another paper was added to the pile before the judge.

The judge tapped the growing pile of papers before her. "It couldn't be an easy case, Mr. Hendricks? Today is my grandson's birthday, and you have to start my day off with a mountain of paper? Well—I suppose it can't be helped. I'll need the remainder of the day to examine these materials. Court is adjourned until nine o'clock tomorrow morning."

Mrs. Macrae, acting like an escorting battleship, stood up and headed for the doors. Emma clung to her arm as if her life depended on it. John, on her other side, tried to take her other arm, only to be shaken off.

Emma gritted her teeth. "What's this in aid of? Am I good enough to be touched now, Mr. Weld? I am my mother's daughter, you remember."

"You are who you are. Not an image of your parents. I got home last night and thought about what you'd said in the car. I'm not like my father, and you don't seem to be like your mother," he said politely. "Would you ladies like me to drive you home?"

"No, thanks,' Emma said, startled at his tacit apology. "Mrs. Macrae drove us down here in the estate car."

"Besides," Mrs. Macrae chimed in, "it has air-conditioning. Your Jeep doesn't. We prefer to travel in comfort!"

"I'm sorry," John said. "I didn't mean to suggest that you travel in less than luxury."

"Well, I don't know," Mrs. Macrae said, falling into the same spirit.

"I tell you what," John said, his eyes sparkling. "To make it up to you, what if I come to dinner tonight?"

"It's up to Emma," Mrs. Macrae said.

"Let me go over that one again," Emma said. "So *you* can make up to me—er—us, *you'll* come to dinner? That's a favor you're doing me?"

"Exactly," he said solemnly. Emma looked around. Mrs. Macrae was grinning like a banshee. John had the look of a choirboy. How do I say no? she asked herself. I want him to be there. It's not entirely his fault that he blamed the Ballentines for all the sorrow of his youth. Or is it? In any event, I *want* him to be there. For dinner, for breakfast, for—Lord, what a fool I've been. And probably will continue to be! "Please come to dinner tonight?" Emma asked, but without a great deal of enthusiasm.

"Thank you for your kind offer," John said with a look that commented on her lack of warmth in the invitation. He was still grinning when the two women made off in their car.

"What do you think happened today?" Mrs. Macrae asked Emma as they drove back to Balleymore with the car air-conditioning working to the maximum.

"I'm not sure," Emma said, still thinking about John's self-invitation to dinner.

"I just hope the judge can see that you're my Emma," Mrs. Macrae said, worried.

"Don't worry, Mattie," Emma reassured her. "Whatever happens, I will always be your Emma."

They finished the ride home in silence. Both were lost in their own thoughts. When Emma stopped the car at Balleymore, Mrs. Macrae asked, "What do you want for dinner?"

"Whatever you decide to cook," Emma hastened to say. "You're the best cook in the county—you decide. It will be perfect. I've got to get to work. I haven't written a word in six days. My editor will want my hide if I don't get something down on paper."

They entered the house and each went her own way, Mrs. Macrae to the kitchen and Emma up to her room and her word processor. Neither was exactly happy at the plans for the rest of the day, but willing to work at them.

Several hours later, Emma came out of her creative trance and looked at the clock. Good grief, she thought. I've been working for nearly six hours. But I've accomplished a great deal. I just have to remember this train of thought. Luke makes a wonderful subject for murder, but I've got too many willing murderers in the wings. I'd really like to stay and think things out but Mrs. Macrae likes an audience for her meals. And John is coming to dinner. John is coming to dinner! She was almost singing the phrase as she dashed into the shower.

When she came downstairs, Mattie met her in the hall. "Oh, you are downstairs," said the housekeeper. "I thought I'd have to come up and drag you down to dinner. I was up about two hours ago and looked in on you. You were pounding away at that contraption and never noticed me. You can certainly concentrate."

"I was hit by inspiration," Emma laughed. "When that happens, the rest of the world disappears for me. I'm sorry if I ignored you."

"That's all right, dear. I have that problem in the kitchen sometimes," the housekeeper said, beaming. "Dinner is ready and your guests are in the dining room, waiting for you. I wasn't going to serve them until you came down."

"My guests?" Emma asked. "Plural?"

"John and Jill and Luke."

"Thank you, Mattie." She leaned over to kiss the elderly cheek. "You are my heroine. This isn't the Ides of March, is it?"

"Not by a long shot. Off with you now," Mrs. Macrae said as she steered Emma toward the door of the dining room.

Not much had changed since the first night Emma had dined there. Luke and Jill were seated over by the window, holding hands. John was standing by the fireplace, apparently waiting for her.

"Well, here you are, finally," Luke said from the couch. "We didn't think Mrs. Macrae was going to feed us without you being here. When Jill inherits we're going to have to turf that woman out of here. Not that we'll be here anyway. We're going to sell this dump and move on to some place exciting. Nothing happens around here."

Emma cringed at the remark. The only thing I can do, she thought, is to stay calm and keep quiet. But it was difficult.

"Don't say that, Luke," Jill protested. "She's been here for most of her life. I think she should get a pension or something."

"If you say so," Luke said with a sneer. "But since we're going to be on the Riviera, what's it matter?"

Despite the early signs, the dinner went very well. Everyone was busy eating Mrs. Macrae's wonderful apple pork chops. Emma complimented Mattie on her cooking and Mattie just smiled. When the last dish was served and eaten, Luke and Jill disappeared from the room with no goodbyes. This left John and Emma alone at the table, seated side by side.

John cleared his throat and said, "I don't know if I should tell you, but it appears that legally you will be named the heir to the estate. I got that from Mr. Hendricks."

Emma sat for a moment not saying anything. "You know," she said, "that's just too bad. I don't really want it." She said this very quietly and then stood up and walked out of the room.

She met Mrs. Macrae in the hall as she was heading for the stairs. "It was an absolutely lovely dinner, Mattie. I'm sorry, but I don't want dessert. I'm going back upstairs to my word processor. I've a living to make."

Emma hurried upstairs and sat down at the word processor. Inspiration was far away and on vacation. All she could think about was life without John. She hated the idea. She had been lonely before but this time it would be worse. She had never known what she'd been missing before. Now she knew.

All I ever wanted, she thought as she sat in front of the word processor, was to be part of a family. To be related to someone. To have someone love me. Well, I do have Mattie. That's a positive result. The problem, as I see it, is I may be the heir and inherit the whole kit and caboodle. But that's money and property. I don't need those things. I want a family. I want John Weld.

Tonight is going to be another sleepless night, isn't it? Oh, well. Get on with it, girl, you've a living to make!

She sat at the processor for an hour and a half just pecking at the keys. Mrs. Macrae knocked at the door and at her invitation came in the room. She was carrying a tray with a pot of coffee, a milk jug, a big piece of chocolate-mousse pie and two cups with saucers.

"Oh," Emma said, feeling an intense love for this woman, "you shouldn't have. But I'm thankful you did. Just put the tray here and pull up a chair."

"I thought you might like this," Mrs. Macrae said as she put the tray down and sank into the chair by the small table. "I hope I'm not disturbing you."

"No," Emma said, "you're not disturbing me. I'm having trouble getting back into the swing of things right now."

"Well," Mrs. Macrae said soothingly, "I'm sure you'll find it soon enough." As she spoke she poured the coffee and added milk to Emma's cup. She handed the coffee to her and passed the pie to her too. She had a look on her face that had Emma wondering. "You know," Mrs. Macrae started hesitantly, "I don't eavesdrop, but every so often I overhear things in this house as I'm going about my duties. I heard you and Mr. John talking. I heard him say that you'd be named the legal heir in court, not that I needed the court to tell me who you are."

"And then," Emma continued for her, "you heard me say that I didn't want it."

"Yes," Mattie said. "Why don't you want Balleymore? You are the only Ballentine left. You should live here, where the Ballentines have lived for generations. You were born here. Your father was born here. All the way back to Micah Ballentine, who was the first to come out here to the Frontier."

"Mattie," Emma said, "I really don't care about having money or property. I earn my own. I came out here to find out who I am. This whole inheritance thing is just confusing the issue."

"You are," Mattie said with conviction, "Emma Elizabeth Ballentine, and none of this is confusing the subject. The property and money is incidental. The important thing is that you will know what I know. And that is, you are *my* Emma. Now eat your pie and finish your coffee and go to bed. Tomorrow is another big day. I'll leave the dishes up here for tonight. You can bring them down tomorrow morning. Good night, my dear." Mattie bent down and kissed Emma's cheek. She left behind the feel of warm lips and love.

The next morning in court Emma noticed two men in the courtroom who hadn't been there yesterday. "Who are they?" she whispered to Mr. Hendricks.

"Those, my dear," Mr. Hendricks said with a laugh in his voice, "are the official tax collectors of both the federal government and the Commonwealth of Massachusetts. In cases where there is a large inheritance at stake, they like to come and find out who inherits. Then they can be sure who they're going to go after." He then turned to face the bench as the judge was announced.

"Let's get going, Counsel," Her Honor said. "Do you have your experts available?"

"Yes, Your Honor," the lawyer said.

The bailiff called the first of the handwriting experts to the stand. After having sworn as to his credentials, he was asked about his findings on the holographic will Emma had brought with her from New York.

"It is," the expert said, "probable that the said document was, in fact, written by Edward Everett Ballentine. I have compared this sample with ten other samples of his handwriting. They match to within ninety-three per cent."

The expert was dismissed and Mr. Hendricks stepped up to the bench once again. "Your Honor," he started. "It seems, after much searching among county records, that the alleged death certificate of E.E. Ballentine as presented by Emma Jill Ballentine is a forgery. There is no record in this county of this alleged death. In fact, Emma Jill Ballentine may be the daughter of an E.E. Ballentine, but not of Edward Everett Ballentine of Balleymore. The document from New York concerning the death of Edward Everett Ballentine is the legal statement."

Jill let out a little gasp. She turned to Luke. "What does he mean? The death certificate is a fake? Where did you get it? You told me there was nothing to worry about! You said I was the daughter. You said I'd inherit." She was talking in a strident whisper and Luke was trying desperately to placate her.

"I don't know what happened," he protested. "I was assured by the private detective I hired that everything was legal and above board. Trust me, Jill. You *are* the heir. Would I lie to you?"

"Ladies and gentlemen," came from the bench, "may we continue? Do you have anything else, Mr. Hendricks?"

"No, Your Honor, this is all we have at the moment."

"It is all rather circumstantial," the judge said thoughtfully. "I'm going to adjourn for the day to let us all think on the subject. Are you sure there isn't anything else that might prove the issue? A birthmark? Some childhood scars? Fingerprints?"

Mr. Hendricks shook his head, but at her words Mrs. Macrae's eyes lit with a certain gleam. When they all exited the courtroom, Mrs. Macrae invited the lawyer to dinner to discuss what else might be used to solve the problem.

On the drive home, Mrs. Macrae sat lost in her thoughts. Emma decided not to try and intrude on them. When they got home, Mattie disappeared into the kitchen. This was fine with Emma, as she thought she might once again find her inspiration.

Several hours later, the housekeeper came into the room and touched Emma on the shoulder. "Good grief," Emma said. "You startled me. I wasn't expecting it. Let me get my heart back down into my chest and I'll be right with you." After a few seconds of deep breathing, she continued, "Is something wrong?"

"No, nothing's wrong. It's dinnertime. I hope you don't mind, but I've invited Dr. Owens to dinner tonight too."

"No," Emma said, "I don't object. I just hope he gets to finish his meal this time."

"He will," Mrs. Macrae said rather cryptically. "Just get ready for dinner. I'll be serving in half an hour."

"Yes, ma'am," Emma said with a smile.

She was downstairs within twenty-five minutes. She had changed into a pretty green and pink sundress with a large skirt that swirled around her when she turned. She felt, somehow, that she needed the confidence this dress would give her for this evening.

"How pretty you look," the lawyer said.

"Thank you," Emma said as she accepted a glass of white wine from John.

"I can get away with saying it because everyone thinks that I'm too old to remember the game," Mr. Hendricks contributed. "That's wrong, you know. I remember the game and its rules. I just can't remember the *object* of the game."

"I'm fairly sure," Dr. Owens said as everyone laughed, "that there is darn little you've forgotten in your lifetime."

"You might be right," the lawyer said. "One thing I haven't forgotten is that when Mrs. Macrae invites you to dinner you go."

"Is that a hint?" Mrs. Macrae said as she brought out the London broil she was offering for dinner.

"Not so much a hint as a prayer," Mr. Hendricks said. He sniffed heartily, taking in the aroma of the beef, sweet potatoes and vegetable ratatouille.

This was the start of a magical evening for Emma. The conversation and the food were wonderful. Mr. Hendricks and the doctor kept everyone in stitches with stories about cases and personalities they had each met. Both of these gentlemen had a turn of phrase and an eye for the ridiculous. The dinner ended on another high note. Mrs. Macrae brought out the dessert. She had made a chocolate layer cake with chocolate icing.

"It's called 'Death by Chocolate,'" Mrs. Macrae said as the diners sat in awe of this calorific masterpiece. She proceeded to cut and hand out the cake so that everyone had a piece.

Emma loved chocolate. She made a promise to herself that she'd not touch another piece of chocolate until May of next year. But this looked scrumptious! And May was such a long time away.

Mrs. Macrae and the doctor both watched as Jill and Emma each ate their piece of cake. Jill took a big forkful and very carefully bit a piece off. She added a look of ecstasy that pierced her makeup, and took a bigger bite.

Emma took a small bite and enjoyed the taste going down her throat. And then she started to feel very uncomfortable. She couldn't breathe. Her eyes started to water and puff. Hives popped out all over her arms, her face, all over her body! She couldn't even swallow the water she reached for urgently. And then she lost consciousness, falling face forward into the remainder of the cake slice she had coveted.

"You wanted proof," Mrs. Macrae said victoriously as she gently pulled Emma's face out of the cake. "Here's the proof. Doctor, you'd better give her the medicine. I put peanut butter in the cake. My Emma is allergic to peanut butter. Dr. Owens' records showed that. I *knew* this was my Emma!"

Jill, unaffected by the cake, took one more big bite and then put her fork down and folded her hands in her lap. A tear formed at the corner of her eye.

CHAPTER NINE

"WHAT have you done to her?" John asked Mrs. Macrae angrily as he jumped to his feet, knocking his chair over backward. "Were you trying to kill her?"

"Calm down, John," Mr. Hendricks said. "I believe Mrs. Macrae has taken care of a major problem." He then looked over at the housekeeper and smiled. "However, did you have to take the name of the dessert, good as it is, so seriously?"

Dr. Owens was giving Emma an injection as they talked. "Not to worry, folks," he said. "She'll be coming around very soon. This is not as serious as it may look." He looked over at Jill and asked, "How are you feeling? Any reactions?"

Jill had a rather dumbfounded look on her face as she shook her head. Luke, on the other hand, was looking suddenly sobered. "What's this?" he almost shouted. "Some kind of trick to try and cheat me out of *my* money?" He stood and glared at the others at the table. "You're all against me!" He got a scheming look in his eyes and said, "I've got to make a phone call." He practically ran out of the door of the dining room and moments later they could hear the roar of his car engine as he raced out of the driveway.

Jill had a questioning look on her face. "*His* money? What did he mean by that?"

No one answered.

Emma started to regain consciousness as Mrs. Macrae wiped her face clean of the cake. "Emma," she said. "Can you hear me?"

Emma tried to open an eye. It was hard to do. She could open her eyes only a slit. "Uh huh."

"I'm sorry, honey," Mrs. Macrae said. "I had to prove that you are my little Emma. I knew about your allergy and I talked Doc Owens into being here with the medicine. I certainly didn't mean to hurt you. I wouldn't ever hurt you! Please forgive me." She was practically in tears by this point. Emma reached out a hand and grabbed Mrs. Macrae's arm.

"What's in the cake?" Emma croaked. The others at the table could see more new hives by the second.

"Peanut butter," John said disgustedly.

"Oh."

"Come on, sweetheart," Mrs. Macrae said coaxingly. "Let's get you up to bed." With John's help, she got Emma to her feet. John gave the housekeeper a sour look then picked Emma up and headed for the staircase.

"Will everybody stay here until I get back, please?" he asked as he went out of the door with Emma in his arms. Mrs. Macrae scurried behind them.

They were both back fairly soon. The doctor and Mr. Hendricks were finishing off their cake and emptying the coffeepot. They seemed to be in very amiable moods. Jill, on the other hand, was sitting at the table with the cake pushed away from her place. She was gripping her water glass with both hands, as if she were choking it to death.

"Is she all right?" Jill asked as John and Mrs. Macrae entered the room.

"She should be," the doctor said. "All she needs now is a good night's sleep and she'll be fine in the morning."

"That's good," Jill said. She very quietly got up from the table and walked out of the room.

John turned to face the doctor and the lawyer. "Perhaps you can explain to me how it is that a medical doctor could let himself be roped into such an affair. Isn't this the *slightest* bit unethical?" The sarcasm ran wild in that question.

"John," the lawyer said, "you are being, perhaps, just a trifle picky in the wording of your question. You will have to admit that this is another piece of the puzzle. It is, perhaps, the key piece of the puzzle."

John didn't care that the doctor had had the medicine on hand or that Mrs. Macrae loved Emma like a grand-daughter. He was finding it hard to protect Emma from others who loved her. Including himself. With these friends Emma didn't need any enemies. Nobody seemed to see that Emma had been in danger.

"If you've finished with the games for tonight, I'm going home," John said. "You've made me so damn mad that I have to go home or I won't be responsible for my actions. I'll be by tomorrow morning to take Emma to court. Have her ready by nine o'clock. And don't try any more experiments!" He stomped out of the dining room and out of the house.

"Well," Mr. Hendricks said as he looked at the two conspirators, "that was a pretty drastic test, wasn't it? Do you think you could do it again tomorrow in court?"

"Don't be silly," the doctor commented. "All we need now is my affidavit."

Emma woke finally, when Mrs. Macrae knocked on the door. "Come in."

The elderly woman came in bearing a tray with coffee and pastries. "Are you all right, dear?" Mattie asked concernedly. "I'm sorry if I scared you, but it was the only way I could think of to prove who you are."

"Mattie," Emma said as she struggled to sit up in bed, "I know you only wanted what's best for me. And, if you were going to feed me peanut butter, I'm glad you didn't tell me beforehand. Just don't do it again, okay?" Her movement in the bed started the itch again. My God, she thought, I swore to myself I'd never have another allergic reaction again. I hate this! I'm going to have to get a pill. "Mattie," Emma asked hesitantly, but with growing urgency, "did Dr. Owens give you a pill for me?" Please say yes, Emma thought.

"Yes," Mattie replied. "Do you want one now?"

"Yes, please," Emma said. The need to scratch was growing worse by the second. It seemed to take ages for Mattie to dig out the pill. I'm going to have to scratch, Emma thought desperately.

Mrs. Macrae gave Emma the pill and watched with a concerned look as she took the pill with one hand and scratched her stomach with the other.

"I didn't realize that this was what Robert Owens was talking about when he was talking about reactions. I'm sorry, honey. Is there anything I can do?"

"You can find me a pair of gloves," Emma said as she stopped scratching. She stopped not because she wasn't itchy. She stopped because it worried Mattie. She would have to scratch on the sly.

"I can do that," Mattie said. "Here, have a cup of coffee."

Jill had, evidently, heard them in Emma's room because she knocked on the door and came in. She was still dressed in her pyjamas, but she looked very, very somber. She looked as if she had been thinking all night, and evidently her thoughts hadn't been pleasant. "I hope you don't mind my coming in," she said hesitantly.

"No," Emma said quickly, "I don't mind. In fact, do you want coffee? Mattie has certainly brought enough of it. I think we have an extra cup. Come on over and sit down on the bed. We can sit, drink coffee and stuff ourselves with pastries."

Jill was quick to join in the proposed program and when Mattie came back with a pair of rubber gloves all three of the ladies enjoyed their coffee and baked goods.

"It doesn't look as if Luke is going to take me to the courthouse today. Could I get a ride with you?" Jill's question sounded a little shaky.

"Mr. John will give you a ride when he comes for Emma and me," Mrs. Macrae promised.

"Is Mr. John giving us a ride today?" Emma asked as she swallowed that last piece of pastry.

"You're not in any shape to drive."

"I feel all right," Emma protested. "And I don't want to impose on—Mr. Weld."

"But you look," Jill said, "*bad*."

"You don't approve of this look?"

"Well, to be honest, I wouldn't choose it. I guess you haven't looked in a mirror this morning."

"No," Emma said, "I haven't. Are you suggesting that I avoid mirrors today?"

"If I were you," Jill said, "*I would*."

I could get to like this, Emma thought as she and Jill bantered. I guess that this is what having a sister is like. I guess if I got to choose my sister I might choose Jill. Why not?

Emma got up out of bed and went toward the bathroom. When she saw herself in the mirror, she groaned. "I should have taken your advice, Jill. Look at my face."

"And your arms and your legs," came her reply from Jill's room. "You take your shower first. I've got to decide what to wear today."

"Thanks," Emma said. "I'll be quick."

She lived up to her word and was out of the shower in record time. Now to figure what to wear. What went well with hives? Something polka-dotted? Perhaps a plaid? Just pick something, she told herself. If he's going to be here by nine o'clock I've got to be ready. I've got to find something that is not only long-sleeved but cool at the same time.

She finally decided on a pale lavender long-sleeved gauze shift with darker purple flowers used as a print on the material. It was lined with a pale lavender slip that covered her torso. It was light, comfortable, and it didn't cling to her body at any point. She had hives on the tops of her feet too, so she was wearing leather thong sandals that strapped around her big toe.

When she got to the foot of the stairs, she met both Mrs. Macrae and Jill. "Are we ready to go out and face the world?" Emma asked.

"As ready as we'll ever be," said Mrs. Macrae as she handed Emma the promised pair of gloves. She was wearing a flowered skirt with a pink short-sleeved cotton blouse and canvas shoes. Jill was dressed in another sundress. It was very bright and much cheerier than Jill looked this morning.

Promptly at nine o'clock the ladies saw the Jeep drive up in front of the house. They went out. "My goodness," John said, trying very hard not to look at Emma's face. "Three ladies all ready on time. Will miracles never cease?"

"Watch out, buddy," Emma said. "We outnumber you. Who is to say that we don't hijack this vehicle and leave you by the side of the road?"

John was delighted to hear the laughter in Emma's voice. Her face was marked with three spots, one on her chin, one on her forehead and the other on her right cheek. It was better than last night when he had taken her upstairs. And thank God for that, he murmured.

The drive to the courthouse was done with laughter and care. John was particularly cautious not to mention that he'd seen neither hide nor hair of his brother, Luke, since last night. He had been almost afraid to look in his petty-cash drawer at home. He had the feeling that it was probably empty.

When they arrived at the court, the four of them went to the door of the familiar courtroom, where the bailiff welcomed them and let them in to wait for both the judge and Mr. Hendricks.

Mr. Hendricks was five minutes late. He entered the court from the judge's door and came to sit down at his place. The judge entered about two minutes later. They quickly came to order.

"Have you any more evidence for the court, Mr. Hendricks?"

"Yes, Your Honor," the lawyer said. "I call Mr. William Blanchard to the stand."

Mr. Blanchard, a slim, dapper man of about forty, took the stand and the questioning began.

"What is your name and occupation?"

"My name is William X. Blanchard. I'm a private detective."

"You have information that concerns this case?"

"Yes, ma'am. I was hired by the Ballentine estate to check on the veracity of certain legal documents which have been presented to this court."

"And your findings?"

"I was looking for a death certificate alleged to have been recorded in this county. The alleged death certificate was that of Edward E. Ballentine, supposed to have died on April 16, 1985 in this county. There is no record of such a death certificate having been entered into the court records. In fact, the doctor's signature affixed to said document was forged."

Jill turned white. "He told me that my father was Edward E. Ballentine. Luke told me my father was the owner of Balleymore. He told me he had the death certificate," she whispered, agitated.

"Have you anything else to say to the court on this matter, Mr. Blanchard?" the judge asked.

"Yes, Your Honor," Mr. Blanchard said. "When I found the document was a forgery, I went to the police with my findings."

"Have the police acted on your findings?" the judge asked.

"Yes, Your Honor."

"Thank you for your time and testimony, Mr. Blanchard. You may step down."

The judge quickly called the police who were present in the courtroom to the stand. The policeman who came forward was dressed in plainclothes and swore himself in as Police Detective James Hartwell. "Your Honor, on receiving evidence from Mr. Blanchard about the forgery attempt we investigated the case. We went to Springfield and found the forger. We were quite lucky in that, Your Honor. We have him in the courtroom, if you wish to speak to him."

The forger turned out to be a seedy little man wearing a dirty brown cardigan and wool pants. Emma perspired just looking at him.

"My name is Peter J. Donovan, Your Honor." This was said in a thin voice with the air of someone who'd been here before.

"Mr. Donovan, the crime of forgery is a serious one. This court cannot hear your case, but it may go easier for you if you could tell us who commissioned your talents in this case."

"You got me to rights," Mr. Donovan said. "The guy who hired me said there'd be no problems. Just make up the death certificate and don't worry. There ain't no other heirs and the money's just lying there. Ain't it my luck?"

"Could you give us a name, Mr. Donovan?"

"Sure," Mr. Donovan said. "Luke Weld. That guy's brother." He pointed to John. He looked at the people sitting behind Mr. Hendricks and he saw Jill. "Say, ain't you the gal Weld was trying to get money from? Ain't it just my luck? He told me we'd make a bundle and no one'd know. So here I am and where's he? Probably taking a vacation in Brazil."

Jill said nothing. She sat in her chair and cringed. Emma felt sorry for her. She put her arm around the smaller girl's shoulders.

Mr. Donovan was dismissed from the stand and remanded back into the hands of the police.

"I authorize a warrant for the arrest of Luke Weld. I take it he is not present at this time?" The counsel nodded and the judge continued, "Is there anything else you'd like to bring before the bench for this case, Mr. Hendricks?"

"Yes, Your Honor," Mr. Hendricks said. "Last night, while at dinner with the two claimants, Mr. John Weld,

Mr. Luke Weld and Dr. Robert Owens, Mrs. Edna Macrae served a chocolate cake which had been made with a portion of peanut butter. According to Dr. Owens' records the child of Edward Everett and Emma Julia Ballentine was violently allergic to peanut butter. The claimant named Emma Elizabeth suffered a severe reaction to the peanut butter cake. Claimant Emma Jill Ballentine suffered no reaction at all from eating the same cake. This is an affidavit from Dr. Owen. He witnessed the action and treated the patient. If Your Honor wishes, we could reproduce the experiment in court."

Jill stood up suddenly. "No," she said very clearly, "I don't think we have to do that test again. I'm not the daughter of Edward Everett and Emma Julia Ballentine. I was just kidding myself that what Luke told me was right. It's not mine. I'm an orphan without a name." She was crying.

"I'm afraid," the judge said, "Miss Emma Jill Ballentine, that all of the proof in this case upholds your contention of not being the heir." She banged her gavel and then said, "The court of the Commonwealth of Massachusetts finds for Emma Elizabeth Ballentine as the legal heir and beneficiary of the Ballentine estate. This court is adjourned."

Mrs. Macrae and John both leaned down and congratulated Emma. Emma sat in her seat as if she were glued. She was stunned by the rapid outcome. She was also beginning to itch fiercely. I knew, I thought, when Mattie explained last night that I was truly the daughter of the house. Oh, my God. Don't scratch yourself so hard or you'll leave scars. Why am I not excited about being named the heir? Other than I'm in pain, of course. I should be excited. This reaction is worse than any I've ever had before.

This verdict gives me a past. It gives me a name. It gives me a family and a future. What it doesn't do is give those same things to Jill. I almost wish I could trade places with her. She could have the estate and the hives. I'll be homeless and nameless—and itchless! I know what she's feeling. I've been there. When she said she was an orphan without a name, I knew the feeling. Look at her. She's sitting next to me trying to smile and be brave. This woman is as close to me as if she were my sister. Please, Lord, just make the itching go away!

"What's the matter?" Mrs. Macrae asked Emma. "Are you in pain?"

"I don't know if it qualifies as pain," Emma said. "I am itching all over. I'm probably going to be scratching myself constantly. Thank you for the gloves."

"I'm sorry," Mrs. Macrae said, "I honestly didn't know it would be this kind of reaction. Bob said to take one pill every six hours. Do you want another pill?"

As if she'd been offered the crown jewels, Emma grabbed the tiny pill from Mrs. Macrae's hand. She dry-swallowed the pill and prayed for instant relief while wincing at the acidic taste of the medicine. "You're a lifesaver, Mattie. Thank you." Then the stray word caught her attention. "Who is Bob?"

"Bob?" Mrs. Macrae said as she blushed. "Bob is Dr. Owens. I've known him most of my life. I went to school with him, so I get to call him Bob."

Emma didn't believe that was the whole story. Why should she get embarrassed at calling an old friend by his first name? There was something going on here that she didn't see.

"Ladies," John said to the three women, "are we ready to go back to Balleymore for the celebration feast?"

"Feast?" Mrs. Macrae said. "I don't have time to cook for a party."

"Not to worry," John said. "I called Barbara Hardy, the minister, with the news and she offered to get the party together. It won't be as good as what you can do, but everyone has to make sacrifices."

"I suppose," Mrs. Macrae said. She did look pleased.

All three of the women rose from their chairs. Jill looked troubled, as if she was making a difficult decision. "Can you give me a ride to the bus station after I pick up my things?" she asked John.

"Why do you want to leave?" Emma asked before John could respond.

"I don't have any place here any more," Jill said. "I have to move on."

"Where are you going?" Emma asked.

"Wherever I can get with the money I have," Jill said. "I can get a job wherever that is and earn enough to move on again."

"That sounds very lonely," Mrs. Macrae said with real concern in her voice.

"I'm used to it," Jill said with resignation.

"Well," Emma said, "come back to Balleymore with us and stay for the party. You can decide later."

The four of them got into the Jeep and drove back. They arrived at Balleymore and drove around the back where Reverend Hardy had set up a large barbecue grill and pressed several men into aiding and abetting. The grill was going full burn. There were grilling steak, ribs and chicken. There was a smaller grill with hamburgers and hot dogs for the children. There were about fifty people at the party and more kept coming. Emma recognized some of the people from the funeral. They were estate employees and tenant farmers, complete with their families. It was a holiday, evidently, on the Ballentine estate. To celebrate, the minister had organized a potluck barbecue. Everyone brought a dish to the party.

"There's enough food here to feed the whole valley," Mattie gasped.

Reverend Hardy saw them get out of the car. She came over to welcome Emma home. "Congratulations, my dear. I thought we'd all have a small get-together to welcome you home as the Ballentine heir. I knew that there was no way to compare anything I cooked to Mrs. Macrae's cooking, so I cheated. Come on over, the guests want to welcome you back." She took Emma by the hand and led her over to the group that was gathering.

Emma felt complete, almost. There was something missing. She knew that she'd find the missing part soon. She just didn't know what it was, at this moment. "Thank you all for coming," she said to the crowd who faced her.

"Miss Ballentine," one of the older men addressed her, "my name is Thomas Sullivan. On behalf of the tenants and employees here, we'd like to welcome back the Ballentine heir."

"Mr. Sullivan," Emma started—then it came to her. She knew what was missing. "On behalf of the Ballentine heirs, I'd like to thank you all for coming to welcome us home. My sister and I are very grateful to have you all as friends."

There was a moment of silence while the guests tried to assimilate her words.

"I want all of you," Emma said as she pulled Jill beside her, "to welcome Jill Ballentine, my sister, to our family home."

John and Mrs. Macrae started the applause and it caught quickly. Jill was both startled and then embarrassed. She pulled at Emma's sleeve and said, "What are you doing?"

"I'm adopting you," Emma said. "Keep on smiling."

"You can't do that," Jill said with hope springing in her voice, "can you?"

"Who's going to tell me I can't?" Emma said to her very seriously. "I want you to be at home here. I want you to be part of my family. I've never had a family. Will you be my sister?"

"Yes. You're not selling, are you?" Jill said.

"I have no intentions of selling. I don't need the money, but I need a home."

"Money," Jill said solemnly, "is not the answer to everything, I'm beginning to realize. I thought it would be. It brought me Luke. He introduced me to a side of life and a style of life I'd never even imagined. I liked it. At least, I thought I did. Maybe I was just trying to keep up with Luke. I thought he was the answer to all my dreams. Boy, was I wrong!"

"Anybody could have been dazzled by Luke Weld," Emma said. "He's just the type to play Prince Charming."

"Unfortunately," Jill interrupted, "once you get to know him, you find out he's a frog. A frog with no morals. He conned me out of the money I'd borrowed from the estate after your mother died."

John had been eavesdropping. "He took the whole five thousand dollars?"

"Everything," Jill said. "He said there were some legal costs. I had no reason to distrust him so I gave it all to him."

Emma was ready to eat and she'd rather eat than go over Luke's inadequacies. The pastries early this morning had worn off. She stepped up to the grill and was handed a plate.

"What would you like, boss lady?" the young man at the grill asked as he smiled at her.

"I think I'll start with some chicken," she said. After a breast of barbecued chicken was put on her plate she wandered over to the tables with the salads and other dishes. She got a piece of sweet corn, some macaroni salad, some green salad, and, of course, some potato salad. With her plate filled, another young man showed her one of the seats of honor. They had quickly made a duplicate seat of honor for Jill, the other Ballentine daughter.

Jill, John, Mrs. Macrae, Dr. Owens and Mr. Hendricks all joined her shortly. They all appeared hungry. The only conversation taking place was asking for the salt and butter.

Emma was tempted to go back for seconds, but she saw the desserts being brought out to the tables. Some of the desserts looked absolutely scrumptious. Of course, I'm going to make sure, Emma thought, that none of them has peanut butter in it.

The six people at the head table sat, replete with food. They were resting before dessert. Somehow or another Reverend Hardy had organized some of the younger people into service crews. They came and cleared tables and brought coffee to those who wanted it.

"Are you all enjoying yourselves?" the minister asked the head table. At their groans of pleasure, she continued, "I have the chapel open for weddings on Thursdays. Can I book you, Mrs. Macrae, and you, Doc Owens in for this next Thursday?"

"What are you talking about?" Dr. Owens said, startled.

"Please," Reverend Hardy said. "You two have been playing games for nearly forty years. It's time to stop. Time to shoot pool or whittle." She then turned to Emma and John and with a raised eyebrow said, "Shall I plan for a double wedding while I'm at it?"

Emma was startled. Where did Reverend Hardy get such a thought? Not that Emma hadn't thought about it, she just didn't think anyone else would think about it.

"Just a minute, Reverend," John said. "I think this calls for a private discussion between Emma and myself." He looked at Emma with a half smile. "Would you come with me for a small chat?"

Emma nodded and took his outstretched hand as he led her around the house to the big tree with the bench around it. He seated her on the bench and said, "What are your plans for the next fifty years or so?"

"I haven't really planned that far ahead yet," she whispered. "Just up to the day after tomorrow."

"May I ask what you've planned so far?" John said.

"I've decided to ask you for the name of a reliable person to manage the Ballentine estate. That is, now that you're no longer the conservator. You want to go back to your own land. Balleymore has taken more than enough of your time." Emma said all of this looking over the valley. She didn't want to look at John. It hurt to look at him. He didn't love her. He'd never forgiven her for being a Ballentine.

"Actually," John started—and then stopped. "I've got someone in mind," he continued, "but I'm not sure you'd agree with the suggestion."

"Who is it?" asked Emma.

"Well," John drawled the word, "he has lots of experience with farming. He's a local boy. He's considered to be a whiz at crop selection and harvesting. He's a proven manager."

"This guy," Emma said, "is beginning to sound like the ideal person. Who is he?"

"His name is John Nichols Weld," John said.

"That's you!"

"Yes."

"So it's true," Emma said from between clenched teeth. "You were making up to me only to get to my property."

"I don't want your property," John said as he reached out and grabbed the back of her neck, drawing her closer. "I want you." He brought her even closer and bent down to kiss her. The kiss quickly got out of hand. He had meant to be gentle. She infuriated him at times. At times she excited him out of his wits. Whenever he kissed her it was an experience to be remembered. This was one of those times. "Is this the job interview?" he asked breathlessly.

"You've got the job," Emma breathed as her lips traced his cheekbones.

"Both of them?" John asked.

"Both of them," she said. "I've been talking like a fool, worrying about the money."

"And now?"

"I don't care about the money. I never did. All I want is you."

"There's my girl," John Weld said. "Emma Elizabeth Weld. I like that."

"So do I," she returned as she cuddled up into his shoulder.

When he kissed her, the crowd cheered.

CHAPTER TEN

EMMA was more than willing to stay right where she was, in John's arms. She'd never imagined such happiness. The only problem she could see for the future was that she melted like an ice cube whenever he touched her. That was, if someone wanted to call that a problem.

"I could do this all night," John murmured, "but you have guests."

"Let Jill take care of them," she said as she ran her tongue around his lips. "That's what sisters are for."

"Jill," he said, between little kisses on her neck and earlobes. "Your sister, Jill?"

"Yes." Emma pulled back in his arms. "There may be no blood relation, but we are sisters. Please, don't argue with me on this."

"No," John said very seriously, "I wasn't going to argue about that. I wasn't going to do any arguing. I'm just very sorry that she got caught up with Luke."

"Pretty faces and smooth manners are potent weapons," Emma said.

"Is that why you fell for me?" John asked.

"Not a chance," Emma replied quickly. She laughed and nestled under his chin again before climbing to her feet. "Come on," she said. "Let's go see *our* guests."

The guests were interested in the outcome of the conversation, even though they couldn't hear it. They were pleased to see the two of them come back hand in hand, smiling.

177

"Well," Dr. Owens said, "have you two decided your futures?"

John went over to the table where Dr. Owens and Mrs. Macrae sat. He leaned over and in a loud stage whisper he said, "Yes. Emma and I have decided to take Barbara Hardy up on her offer for the chapel. And what are you going to do? It's a bad example for the younger generation when our elders sneak around in corners to see each other."

The crowd grew quiet. Everyone, except Emma, was aware of the relationship Edna Macrae and Robert Owens had been conducting over the years. Someone called from the back, "Don't you think that forty years is long enough to get to know a girl, Doc? Come on. Ask her."

Dr. Owens stood up and scowled at the audience. "I don't need prompting from all of you. I've been asking her to marry me for the last thirty-nine and a half years." He turned to Mattie and smiled down at her. "Edna, my dear, even if you couldn't cook I'd want to marry you. Please say yes."

Mattie looked down at her plate and blushed. She took a deep breath and looked up at her gentleman friend. "Yes," she said very clearly, "I'll marry you, Robert Owens."

Dr. Owens smiled lovingly and bent down to kiss his fiancée. The crowd began to applaud and cheer. When the couple came up for air, everyone began to disperse.

Reverend Hardy strolled over to the two beaming couples and said, "How long is it going to take you to set up a wedding? Remember, I've got Thursdays open for the next month. Call me when you've decided." She then walked over to the cleaning crew to supervise their duties.

Jill came over to congratulate the pair. She looked a little pensive.

"Is something wrong?" Emma asked.

"Nothing," Jill said. "I thought that I'd be the first to be married. I didn't think you were going to beat me out. Just my luck, isn't it? I pick the flashy brother and he dumps me." She was smiling bravely but Emma could sense the dammed tears. She took her in her arms and just held on as Jill cried over lost dreams and illusions.

Not too much later the guests began to gather their children and dishes in preparation for leaving. They came either singly or as family groups to wish both sisters a happy life at Balleymore. By the time most of the guests had left, the cleaning and replacement of used items had been done. There wasn't anything left to clean or pick up. Except for the large barbecue grill with the still burning coal embers, one would never know there'd been a party there.

Mr. Hendricks and his grandson, Michael, left with the promise that should she need expert legal guidance Emma should get in touch with his law firm. He wouldn't plead the case but he could give assistance and advice. "You can invite me to dinner," he said as he walked to his car. "Or maybe I'd better get an invite to Doc Owen's place. That's where the cook will be!"

Soon the only people left were Jill, Emma, John, Mrs. Macrae and Dr. Owens. The doctor went inside with Mrs. Macrae to make a phone call to his practice. Not long afterward, he came out of the house and walked over to the others standing there. "Well," he said, "I've got a few calls to make. I won't be back this evening. I've got an operation scheduled and then I'm on call." He looked back at the house. "Edna is in there making coffee for anyone who wants some. Bye." He walked quickly to his car and soon was pulling out of the driveway.

"I feel like an outsider," Emma said.

"Why?" John asked.

"I never knew Mattie was seeing Dr. Owens," she said. "This whole thing about the two of them was a surprise to me."

"Even I knew about them," Jill commented. "I thought it was cute. You know, at their age and all."

"Well," Emma said. "Let's go inside. It's never too late for loving. I could use a cup of coffee." She started for the door and the other two followed.

John caught her at the door and moved aside to let Jill pass. "I'm going to have to go home," he said. "I *do* have a farm of my own to run."

"Are you planning to run both your own farm and the Ballentine lands?" Emma asked.

"No," John said. "I'm planning to put Jesse Fernandez in charge of the Weld farm and concentrate on you. He's my right-hand man. While I was conservator, that's how I managed. It worked well then and I can't imagine it failing now. I'll probably give him a piece of the business. But anyway, I've got to go take care of some business this evening. It's been a long day. Why don't you go to bed early tonight? I'll be over tomorrow. We can plan the wedding then. Okay?" He kissed her. It was supposed to be a good-night kiss, but it turned serious almost immediately, as usual. "We have to get married quickly," he muttered. "If I can't finish this soon I'll go crazy! Good night, Emma." He backed away abruptly and then turned to march to his Jeep.

Emma could hear him talking to himself as he left. Something about cold showers and abstinence. She laughed with the joy of life and turned to go inside.

* * *

The next morning was cloudy with the promise of rain. I'm praying for rain, Emma thought as she came down the staircase. When she got to the kitchen both Jill and Mrs. Macrae were sitting at the table with coffee cups in hand. It looked as if they were gossiping. Isn't that nice? she thought. My family.

Mattie got up and poured Emma a cup of coffee. "We're having omelets this morning. With ham, green peppers and cheese. If that's acceptable, just nod your head. I know that you're not awake yet, but give it a shot."

"What are you trying to do to me?" Emma asked her oldest friend. "Are you trying to make me laugh so that I wake up quicker? It'll work, believe me."

"Good," Jill chimed in. "We want you awake, as soon as possible."

"Can I ask why?"

"We have to plan two weddings!" Jill said, as if she thought Emma had forgotten.

"Have you and Mattie come to any decisions yet?" Emma asked after she swallowed her first mouthful of coffee.

"Other than who we're each marrying," Mattie said, "nothing has been decided. I get the feeling that Jill wants to organize everything."

"I'm the only family you two have," Jill stated. "I was up late last night thinking over Emma's proposition to adopt me. If she does, and I want her to, you're part of my family. Can I call you Mattie, the way Emma does?" This question was asked rather diffidently.

Mattie's face beamed. "Of course you can. I'd love to have the two young women I love calling me Mattie."

"Thank you," Jill said as she leaned over and kissed Mattie's cheek. "Now, I'm the only one not actively involved in a wedding at the moment. So as the only free Ballentine in the group I'm taking over on the plans for the wedding. Is that all right with you two?''

The other two were amazed at the forceful and purposeful person who now faced them. They just nodded on command.

"Just let me start the omelets," Mattie said, "before we get to the lace and organdie."

"I'm sure we can wait that long," Emma said. "And long enough to eat it with the dedication it deserves. Don't you agree?" She aimed the question toward Jill and was relieved to see a smile.

About halfway through the meal, Jill started to ask wedding questions. "Do you want this to be a double wedding?"

"If you don't mind," Mattie said, "I don't want a large wedding. This will be my second. My first wedding was a large one with the white and all. But that was years ago. I want to get married quietly. I don't want a lot of people there. I talked to Bob earlier and he said we could run off to Nevada if I wanted to."

"If you run off to Las Vegas for your wedding," Emma said, "then it's just that much farther we have to go to attend. Why don't you just have it here? You could have the minister come up here for the ceremony. You don't have to be married in the church building. We could keep it small, couldn't we?" This was asked of Jill.

Jill had been nodding while Emma was speaking. When Emma asked, she said, "Yes. I guess we could. But that means that you and John will get married in the church with the whole works."

"What?"

"Oh, c'mon, Emma," Jill said. "John knows a lot of people. They'll all want to come. Besides, don't you want a big white ceremony?"

I remember the dream, Emma thought, where I walked down the aisle in white. When I got to the altar, there he was—Prince Charming! Well, I've finally got it right. He *is* Prince Charming. "Yes," she said to both Mattie and Jill, "I would like a *real wedding*." She stopped and smiled at her audience and then, "I remember reading somewhere that if someone was planning to get married they would normally have to plan way in advance."

"That may be so for most people," Jill said, glancing at Mattie, "but you have a shortcut through all of the wait."

"I do?" Emma asked. She was confused.

"I don't want to brag," Mattie said. "I've been on the phone to various people in the area. We can get the dresses fitted tomorrow. I'll do the catering. Jill will do the planning and organizing. John only has to worry about getting a ring. You only have to decide when to have the ceremony."

"What about you?" Emma asked Mattie.

"Bob and I want to get married in two weeks," Mattie said. "If we can do it here, that would be wonderful."

"Where will you be living?" Emma asked.

"We haven't decided yet," Mattie said. "Bob sold his house to the new doctor and has been in an apartment. He'd originally made plans to go to Florida when he retired. I think I've talked him out of it."

"If you're going to stay in the area," Emma said diffidently, "would you consider living here at Balleymore? We've plenty of room. Dr. Bob isn't planning to retire for a couple of years, is he?"

"He figured on working at least two more years," Mattie confirmed.

"We'd love to have you both living here in the meanwhile," Emma said.

"I'll have to ask Bob," Mattie said.

The kitchen door swung open. All the ladies could see was a masculine hand palm up with a small box on it. A voice came from the hallway. "I have a special delivery for Ms. Emma Elizabeth Ballentine."

With a big smile, Emma stood up and went to the hand with the box. "Now," she said, "what do you think this could be?"

John opened the door to come in the kitchen. "You promised to be my wife last night," he said. "This, if you take it, is a symbol of our engagement."

Emma opened the little blue box. The ring inside was gorgeous. It was a full half-carat diamond surrounded by emeralds. I love this ring, she thought. I love this man. "I love it," she said as she threw herself into his arms.

"Good," he said. "It was my grandmother Weld's engagement ring. She told me that when I found the right girl, that girl would love the ring. I'm certainly glad to see that she was right."

The day passed quickly. Emma spent the day with John. Whenever anyone else joined them Emma made a point of elevating her ring finger and letting the light spring into prisms on her ring. He brought her back from dinner very late. They had gone to a local restaurant called Chez Massard. They dined on grilled trout *amandine* and drank champagne. It was a magic evening for Emma. John walked her to the front door and kissed her good-night.

"Would you like to come in for some coffee?" Emma asked with more than coffee on her mind.

"No, thank you," John said. "We have to get married quickly." He turned and walked toward the Jeep. He turned about half the distance to say, "I've got to go into Boston tomorrow for the flower market. Would you like to come?"

"I'd love it," Emma said, "but I promised Jill and Mattie that I'd go and try on wedding dresses. Should I tell them we want the ceremony in three weeks?"

"Is that what *we* decided?" John asked rather distractedly. "I must have been out of my mind." He said this almost to himself. "Three weeks! I don't know if I can handle it."

"John," Emma said, "it's only three weeks for the ceremony but we could practice on the honeymoon. If you want."

"Get thee behind me, devil woman," John said. "If I start the honeymoon now, you won't be up for the wedding ceremony."

"What?"

"Up for the ceremony," John said. "As in out of bed—up. I've got to get out of here. Good night, Emma. Take care."

Mattie had been married at Balleymore last week. Emma's dress was ready. Jill had organized the party beautifully. Mattie had been cooking for the last three days. The Weld farms had provided the flowers—roses, of course. The church was decorated. The minister was ready.

In the back of the sanctuary, Emma stood in her white dress with lace veil. Let's get this show on the road, she thought nervously as she waited for her number to be played.

When they'd told Mr. Hendricks of their plans to marry he'd been very happy. "I've stood *in loco parentis* for you long enough, Emma. I'm going to give you away." She'd given in without an argument.

The notes of "Here Comes the Bride" started and Emma moved with Mr. Hendricks to the aisle. The aisle has got longer since I walked it during the rehearsal, Emma thought. The sun is certainly bright. It's enough to blind me. I can't see John. He has come, hasn't he? Where is he? Two steps farther down the aisle, she could see him. She relaxed. This is my brass ring, she thought. My prize. I'm certainly glad I finished the manuscript. How odd! Why am I thinking about the book at this moment? My mind seems to be loose from the rest of me.

John reached out and took her hand. Suddenly, everything came into focus for Emma. This was her time. Her joy. He was her future.

She couldn't remember much about the ceremony. She knew, however, when it was her time to say "I do," and she did. She remembered the kiss. It would have been impossible to forget the kiss. She was sorry that Jill had planned a reception after the ceremony. All that would be wasted time. Good manners sustained her for her part of the celebration.

Jill came over to the happy couple and asked John rather diffidently, "Have you heard from Luke?"

"I haven't heard from him directly," he said. "Do you want to get in touch with him?"

"No," Jill said. "I just want to make sure that I won't run into him in any hurry."

"I heard from a friend that Luke was seen on a passenger ship on the St. Lawrence river."

"He must be trawling for a rich woman," Jill said disgustedly. "Anyway, could you introduce me to that tall dark-haired man over there?" She pointed toward Jesse Fernandez. "He isn't married, is he?"

"No," John said. "He's not married. He says he has plenty of time for that."

"Oh, he does, does he?" Jill said with a smile beginning on her lips. "You don't need to introduce me, then. I know how to go about meeting him."

Emma watched with amazement as Jill stalked Jesse. "How does she do that?" Emma asked herself.

"I think," John said, "she was born with the capability." He stopped and looked around at the guests. The crowd had moved into the other room and the happy couple were by themselves. "Now that we're finally alone and we're finally married, let's get started on that honeymoon." They laughed and ran upstairs to the master bedroom Mattie had cleared out for them.

Later that evening, the guests began to take their leave. They said their compliments and farewells to Jill and Mattie. The newlyweds were nowhere to be seen. The phone rang.

"Yes," the man said. "My name is Lindsey Kimball. I'm Emma Ballentine's agent. May I speak to her?"

Jill had answered the phone. "I'm afraid not," she said. "She got married today. She's left on her honeymoon. Do you want to leave a message?"

"How long will she be gone?" the man asked frantically.

"I don't know for sure," Jill replied. "Probably for fifty years."

"Where did she go?" Emma's agent demanded.

"I don't know," Jill said.

"Oh, this is terrible!" the man moaned. "What am I going to do?"

"What's the matter?" Jill, who was too kindhearted for her own good, asked. "Perhaps I can help?"

"Yes," Mr. Kimball said quickly. "You can tell me where she is."

"Sorry. I can't do that."

"Tell me," Mr. Kimball said in a tone of voice once used by snake-oil salesmen, "has she talked about a book she's writing?"

"Oh," Jill said with comprehension. "You mean the book she mailed out yesterday?"

"She mailed a book to me yesterday?" Mr. Kimball said suspiciously.

"Yes," Jill said, while smiling at her end. "She said she wanted to get it in the mail so that when you called asking about it she could say, 'It's in the mail.'"

Upstairs in the honeymoon suite, John Weld shook himself and stretched upward in the bed. Perspiration rolled off his forehead despite the air-conditioning. Mrs. Weld cuddled up close to him and tried to tease him, to no good result.

"Listen here," he protested. "I've done all I can. How did I get the impression that you were one of those——? Stop that!"

"One of those what?" his very new wife inquired. Her hands roamed over him as if she were playing a Brahms concerto.

"One of those women who sewed a fine seam and let her husband catch his breath now and again."

"I can't sew worth a nickel," she told him. "Nobody told you I had a tiger in my tank?"

One of her hands struck pay dirt. There was a stirring in the male beast at her side. "Just one more," she coaxed. "Just one tiny——!"

He took her in one mad surge of power and frustration and lust. Took her from ground zero to a peak, and then rolled off onto the thick mattress, panting.

"I'll be dead by tomorrow," he mourned.

"I'll have my breath back by then," she assured him. "I'll be able to come and weep at the funeral. I'll miss you, believe me, I will."

"Damn tease," he muttered as he pulled her back on top of him. "I wonder what the world record is?"

There was no answer. His wife was too busy to talk.

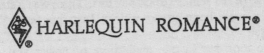

HARLEQUIN ROMANCE®

brings you

Harlequin Romance wishes you a **Merry Christmas...**
with two special Kids & Kisses stories!

**In December, watch for *The Santa Sleuth*
by Heather Allison and *The Nutcracker Prince*
by Rebecca Winters.**

*Romances that celebrate love, families, children—
and Christmas!*

The Santa Sleuth by Heather Allison

Virginia McEnery, age six, is the official "Santa sleuth"
on one of Houston's TV newscasts. Her job is to research
shopping mall Santas. And she whispers her Christmas
wish to every one of them. A *mommy.* Even though her
dad, Kirk, doesn't know it yet, she's already made her
choice—TV news producer Amanda Donnelly.

The Nutcracker Prince by Rebecca Winters

Anna Roberts, age six, wants a *daddy* for Christmas. Her
own daddy. Anna's sure he looks just like the handsome
Nutcracker Prince in her mommy's beautiful book. And
she's right! Because shortly before Christmas, her daddy
appears. His name is Konstantin and he's come here from
Russia. And he wants to marry Meg, her mom....

Available wherever Harlequin books are sold. KIDS7

"HOORAY FOR HOLLYWOOD" SWEEPSTAKES

HERE'S HOW THE SWEEPSTAKES WORKS

OFFICIAL RULES — NO PURCHASE NECESSARY

To enter, complete an Official Entry Form or hand print on a 3" x 5" card the words "HOORAY FOR HOLLYWOOD", your name and address and mail your entry in the pre-addressed envelope (if provided) or to: "Hooray for Hollywood" Sweepstakes, P.O. Box 9076, Buffalo, NY 14269-9076 or "Hooray for Hollywood" Sweepstakes, P.O. Box 637, Fort Erie, Ontario L2A 5X3. Entries must be sent via First Class Mail and be received no later than 12/31/94. No liability is assumed for lost, late or misdirected mail.

Winners will be selected in random drawings to be conducted no later than January 31, 1995 from all eligible entries received.

Grand Prize: A 7-day/6-night trip for 2 to Los Angeles, CA including round trip air transportation from commercial airport nearest winner's residence, accommodations at the Regent Beverly Wilshire Hotel, free rental car, and $1,000 spending money. (Approximate prize value which will vary dependent upon winner's residence: $5,400.00 U.S.); 500 Second Prizes: A pair of "Hollywood Star" sunglasses (prize value: $9.95 U.S. each). Winner selection is under the supervision of D.L. Blair, Inc., an independent judging organization, whose decisions are final. Grand Prize travelers must sign and return a release of liability prior to traveling. Trip must be taken by 2/1/96 and is subject to airline schedules and accommodations availability.

Sweepstakes offer is open to residents of the U.S. (except Puerto Rico) and Canada who are 18 years of age or older, except employees and immediate family members of Harlequin Enterprises, Ltd., its affiliates, subsidiaries, and all agencies, entities or persons connected with the use, marketing or conduct of this sweepstakes. All federal, state, provincial, municipal and local laws apply. Offer void wherever prohibited by law. Taxes and/or duties are the sole responsibility of the winners. Any litigation within the province of Quebec respecting the conduct and awarding of prizes may be submitted to the Regie des loteries et courses du Quebec. All prizes will be awarded; winners will be notified by mail. No substitution of prizes are permitted. Odds of winning are dependent upon the number of eligible entries received.

Potential grand prize winner must sign and return an Affidavit of Eligibility within 30 days of notification. In the event of non-compliance within this time period, prize may be awarded to an alternate winner. Prize notification returned as undeliverable may result in the awarding of prize to an alternate winner. By acceptance of their prize, winners consent to use of their names, photographs, or likenesses for purpose of advertising, trade and promotion on behalf of Harlequin Enterprises, Ltd., without further compensation unless prohibited by law. A Canadian winner must correctly answer an arithmetical skill-testing question in order to be awarded the prize.

For a list of winners (available after 2/28/95), send a separate stamped, self-addressed envelope to: Hooray for Hollywood Sweepstakes 3252 Winners, P.O. Box 4200, Blair, NE 68009.

CBSRLS

OFFICIAL ENTRY COUPON

"Hooray for Hollywood"
SWEEPSTAKES!

Yes, I'd love to win the Grand Prize — a vacation in Hollywood —
or one of 500 pairs of "sunglasses of the stars"! Please enter me
in the sweepstakes!

This entry must be received by December 31, 1994.
Winners will be notified by January 31, 1995.

Name _____

Address _____ Apt. _____

City _____

State/Prov. _____ Zip/Postal Code _____

Daytime phone number _____
(area code)

Account # _____

Return entries with invoice in envelope provided. Each book
in this shipment has two entry coupons — and the more
coupons you enter, the better your chances of winning!

DIRCBS

OFFICIAL ENTRY COUPON

"Hooray for Hollywood"
SWEEPSTAKES!

Yes, I'd love to win the Grand Prize — a vacation in Hollywood —
or one of 500 pairs of "sunglasses of the stars"! Please enter me
in the sweepstakes!

This entry must be received by December 31, 1994.
Winners will be notified by January 31, 1995.

Name _____

Address _____ Apt. _____

City _____

State/Prov. _____ Zip/Postal Code _____

Daytime phone number _____
(area code)

Account # _____

Return entries with invoice in envelope provided. Each book
in this shipment has two entry coupons — and the more
coupons you enter, the better your chances of winning!

DIRCBS